PURRFECT BETRAYAL

THE MYSTERIES OF MAX 11

NIC SAINT

PUSS IN PRINT PUBLICATIONS

PURRFECT BETRAYAL

The Mysteries of Max 11

Edited by Chereese Graves

www.nicsaint.com

Give feedback on the book at: info@nicsaint.com

facebook.com/nicsaintauthor
@nicsaintauthor

First Edition

Printed in the U.S.A

PROLOGUE

The taxi pulled up at the entrance and Camilla got out. The driver darted a curious glance at the gate and cocked an eyebrow in Camilla's direction. "Are you sure about this, honey? Doesn't look like they're expecting you."

He was right, Camilla thought. The gate was closed and the place looked less than inviting. But she'd always known her ex-husband was an eccentric, and it was just like him to invite her to some weird destination for their big reconciliation.

"No, I'll be all right," she said, suppressing a little giggle.

"I guess you know best," said the driver dubiously.

As he drove off into the dark night, she suddenly felt giddy. Nervous, yes, but also excited about the prospect of finally seeing Jeb again. So much had happened in the past couple of months, but if Jeb's texts were to be believed, he considered all of that just water under the bridge.

And she had to admit that when she got those texts, she'd been both surprised and relieved. Surprised that Jeb, after the things she'd accused him of, and the acrimonious battle in the divorce courts, wanted to meet. Relieved that he wasn't holding a grudge, and knew she'd said all of those things simply to get his attention and to make him change his ways. And how else could she have done that than by dragging his name through the mud?

The important thing was that her plan had worked.

He'd finally realized he needed to make a change or lose her forever.

And now she was ready to throw herself into his arms and love him again.

She took a deep breath and stepped up to the gate. And as she did, it swung open with a little click and she directed a smile at the camera mounted on top. Jeb had been watching her. He'd anticipated her arrival as eagerly as she'd anticipated this fated reunion.

She straightened her shoulders, tugged at her silk Donna Karan blouse, and stepped through the gate.

As she did, the gate noiselessly closed behind her and she paused for a moment, getting her bearings.

A driveway led to a hulking mansion that rose up spookily in the distance, backlit by a rising moon. To her immediate left, a smaller brick structure was visible. Inside, the lights were blazing. She smiled. It was just like Jeb to organize their first meeting in months at a place like this. A gamekeeper's lodge, probably, or a renovated custodian's house. She knew why he wanted to meet her here and not at the manor. Nosy staff could spoil their reunion before it even started. Butlers and housekeepers and maids would spread the news, and even before Jeb had opened his arms to clasp her to his bosom, the whole world would know that the divorce of the decade was about to lead to the romance of the century.

It was for the same reason she hadn't used her real name when getting a cab, just like Jeb had advised in his last text, before she boarded her plane at LAX. Tabloids had spies everywhere, and neither she nor Jeb needed some nasty pap suddenly sticking his nose in.

She walked up to the front door of the lodge and held up her hand to knock on the door. Even before it landed on the coarse wood, the door swung open, and she found herself staring at that familiar face.

❧

Jeb woke up with a groan. His head was pounding and his eyes were sore. He rubbed them then stretched. Instantly, he regretted not having stayed perfectly still. The room was spinning so fast he felt like he was on a merry-go-round and about to fall off. His poor suffering stomach lurched, anxious to regurgitate its contents and deposit it on the bed.

He opened his eyes to glare at the offending sun, which had had the gall to intrude upon his fitful sleep.

Sleep, or near-coma.

It had been another long night, and as he sat up in bed he brushed aside an empty bottle of Smirnoff. It fell to the faux sheepskin rug below with a dull clunking sound.

The ashtray was filled to overflowing with cigarette butts and roaches and his bong was still firmly lodged between his thighs.

He was dressed in only his boxers, his fifty-five-year-old body displaying so many tats it was as if a mad tattoo artist had been given free rein to fill up the canvas as he saw fit.

On the nightstand a mirror still held a line of coke, which he now snorted up eagerly, rubbed the remains into his gums and washed it down with a swig from a bottle of Bud.

It was only then that he noticed his hands were covered in some type of weird substance. He stared at it. A dark, reddish brown. Henna? He brought his index finger to his nose and sniffed. In spite of the coke wreaking havoc on his nasal cavities, he frowned when he got a hit of a coppery odor. He gave his finger a tentative lick. Huh. Tasted like blood.

Had he suffered a nosebleed last night? He picked up the mirror, blew off the remnants of white powder and held it up in front of him. Nope. No sign of a nosebleed.

He stared at himself. Once he'd been handsome—every teenage girl's dream. Now he looked like a garden gone to seed. Wisps of dirty grayish hair covered the lower portion of his haggard face, and the eyes that stared back at him were heavy-lidded and tired.

He grinned at himself, and thought not for the first time that he should really pay a visit to the dentist.

As he got up, suddenly something fell to the floor.

He stared at it numbly.

It was one of those big butcher knives.

And it was bloodied.

Weird. Had he cut himself last night? But then why wasn't he in any pain?

He quickly checked himself for holes in his corpus and found none.

Nope. Everything was still as it should be.

He then stumbled out of the bedroom and into the living quarters of the modest lodge he now called home.

And that's when he saw it—or rather, her: lying spread-eagled on his living room rug was the body of a woman. And not just any woman. He instantly recognized her as the woman he'd once loved and had recently divorced in one of the nastiest divorces in Hollywood history.

What was worse, from the way Camilla's lifeless eyes stared back at him, and the spots of dark crimson covering her torso, it was pretty obvious that she was dead.

And that's when the pounding on the door began. And

even before he could rouse himself from the sense of stupefaction that had descended upon him, the door slammed open and a fat cop burst through. The copper took one look at the dead body, then at a bedraggled Jeb, hands bloodied and eyes unfocused, and his expression turned grim.

"Jeb Pott, I'm arresting you on suspicion of the murder of your ex-wife."

CHAPTER 1

I woke up from the sound of distinct mewling. Not so unusual, you might say, since I live in a house occupied by no less than four cats—though technically three of those cats live next door, even though they do spend an awful lot of time at Odelia's. But this mewling was different than the usual sounds my three feline friends Dooley, Harriet and Brutus make. This was more like the mewling of... kittens. And since to my knowledge Odelia has not and hopefully will never take in kittens, this struck me as particularly odd.

Discounting the sound and ascribing it to a bad dream, I attempted to go back to sleep, turning over to my other side at the foot of Odelia's bed, closing my eyes once more.

But the mewling persisted.

With a frown, I pricked up my ears.

No mistake. It definitely was mewling, and it seemed to come from downstairs.

With a sigh of extreme reluctance, for I love to sleep, I dragged my blorange self up from the soft, warm, comfy comforter, and dropped to the hardwood floor below.

My human wasn't up yet, judging from the even breathing, only interrupted by an occasional snuffle, coming from the tousled head on the other end of the bed. And neither was my human's significant other, police detective Chase Kingsley, who was sleeping in the buff, as usual, and had wrestled free from the comforter to display his chiseled torso while his equally chiseled face was frowning. It would appear that even when sleeping Chase was solving crimes and apprehending criminals. The lone warrior of the law never sleeps.

Nor do cats, actually. Not completely, anyway. There's always a tiny part of our consciousness that stays wide awake, ready to pounce on prey, or thwart a natural enemy.

Or track strange mewling sounds where no strange mewling sounds should be.

As I plodded down the stairs, I was already figuring out ways and means.

It could be Odelia's smartphone, which had adopted a new ringtone.

It could be Nickelodeon, launching into its daily programming.

Or it could me, hearing things that weren't here. Though that was highly unlikely.

Behind me, Dooley sleepily muttered, "Wassup, Max. Why you up?"

"Go back to sleep, Dooley," I said. "It's probably nothing."

I may not be one of those guard dogs humans like to keep, but I do possess a certain sense of responsibility, and like to think that in case of danger I'm ready to sound the alarm.

The noise seemed to come from the modest hallway, where Odelia keeps her small cabinet containing knickknacks, her key dish, and an assortment of cat toys locked up safe and sound inside. I know how to jiggle the door, so each time I want to lay my paw on some rubber duck or plastic mouse, it's right there for me to find. Not that I'm all that interested in rubber ducks or plastic mice, mind you. I mean, how old do you think I am? Six months? I'm a grownup, and rubber ducks lost their strange and fascinating appeal a long time ago.

I trod up to the door and put my ear against it. On the other side of the plywood I detected the distinct sound of cats mewling. And not just any cats, either. Kittens. Perhaps the foulest creatures in existence, though that particular and dubious honor should probably go to puppies.

I frowned. What were a bunch of kittens doing on Odelia's doorstep?

"What do you want?" I asked therefore, not making any effort to conceal my disapproval at what amounted to an early-morning raid.

But the mewling continued unabated.

"Oh, stop it, you whiny little pests," I sternly declared. "Just go away and don't come back. This house has plenty of felines and no use for more." Especially—*gasp!*—kittens.

And then I stepped away from the door and fully intended to retreat upstairs and put in another couple of hours of invigorating and refreshing sleep.

You may think me unnecessarily harsh, but you would be wrong. Kittens are a menace, plain and simple, and if you don't believe me just try adopting one. They may seem deceptively appealing, with their cute little faces, and their cute little gestures, and their cute little noises, but I'm here to tell you they're pure, unadulterated evil. Once they get past those first natural defenses, humans will take them in and give them a place, not only in their homes but in their hearts, and soon they won't be able to get rid for them. And since I already have three other housemates to contend with, this was simply a matter of survival.

But as I turned on my heel, I almost bumped into Odelia, who was rubbing the sleep from her eyes.

"Wassup?" she muttered, taking a leaf out of Dooley's book.

"Nothing to concern yourself with," I said. "Go back to sleep."

"No, but I heard something. Is that... a cat?"

"Nope. Not a cat," I said. "Not a cat at all. And I should know, being a cat and all."

"But—"

"No buts. Let's go back upstairs. You and I both need our beauty sleep."

But I could tell the strange fascination the kitten exerts was already working its pernicious magic, for Odelia stepped to the door, arm outstretched, going for the knob.

"Noooooo!" I yelled, but too late.

Already her hand was turning the knob and opening the door.

And there they sat: three kittens, in a carton box, right on our doorstep.

"Oooh!" said Odelia, crouching down. "Ooooooh! Look at those cuties!"

Crap. Even before I could intervene, the poison had entered the bloodstream.

Odelia had spotted the kittens and had gone kitty gaga.

CHAPTER 2

"Who could have put them here?" Odelia asked.

I could very well have asked her the same thing. I, for one, had never given permission to have my home infested by the pesky little pests.

"Isn't there a letter or a card?" I asked.

Odelia, who'd taken the box inside and closed the door, checked for a sign of ownership of the threesome.

She took out a tiny slip of paper and read the message it contained. "I hope you will take good care of my babies. For reasons I cannot disclose, I no longer can. I'm sorry."

She'd placed the box on the kitchen counter and took out the first kitten. It was a ginger specimen, with little white dots, and mewled piteously.

I could tell that Odelia's heart melted even more, for she started making weird sounds herself now. *"Googoogagagoo-goo,"* she said. *"Booboobeebeebooboo."*

I rolled my eyes. Humans tend to lose their heads when they see a kitten. Of course this fatal appeal is exactly the reason our species has endured and has been adopted into the home of no less than one out of three American families: we know how to entice.

"Googoodoodooweeweewoowoo," Odelia said.

The kitten, which had been wriggling, suddenly focused its tiny eyes on Odelia, then produced its first real meow. Gibberish, of course, but still a sign of recognition. Cat, meet cat lady. Cat lady, meet cat.

Odelia laughed. "Hello there, little one. So who put you in a box and left you on my doorstep, huh?"

The kitten meowed some more, then licked its lips. It started looking around, and I could tell it was already adapting to its new home. Uh-oh. It was wriggling and squirming.

"You want to explore my home?" asked Odelia.

I could have told her this was a bad idea, but she was already putting the kitten down and we both watched as it hobbled off at an awkward and unbalanced gait towards the first potted plant it could find. It then climbed into the terracotta pot and relieved itself.

And Odelia, instead of rectifying this behavior with word and gesture, laughed!

She now picked up the two other kittens and cuddled them, rocking them in her arms. One was a velvety black and the third one pure white.

"Oh, you sweet little cuties," Odelia cooed. "Sweet sweeties. Did your mama leave you? Couldn't she take care of you? Don't you worry about a thing. Odelia is here and she's going to make sure nothing bad happens to you." And then she googoogaga'd some more.

I could sense that smarter heads needed to prevail here, so I addressed Kitten Number One, the whizz kid.

"Hey, you," I said, inserting a note of steel into my voice.

The kitten didn't even look up from sniffing at its own wee.

"Don't pretend you can't hear me. I know you can."

The kitten finally looked up, opening its mouth and mewling questioningly.

"There are rules in this house," I said. "And you'd better follow them or else."

It was mewling softly now, opening and closing its little mouth.

"Or else what, you ask? Or else I'll tan your tiny little hide, that's what."

"Max!" Odelia cried behind me. "That's no way to speak to our new guests."

"But—"

"Apologize."

I must admit my jaw had dropped at these harsh words from one I'd always known to be in my corner. The kitten fever had clearly taken a hold of my human, and had altered her personality to such an extent she was now a different human altogether.

"I'm sorry," I told the kitten begrudgingly.

"And now say it like you mean it," said Odelia.

"Okay, I'm sorry, all right!" I cried, then stalked off. Or at least I started stalking off, but then my tail got snagged in some immovable object and my progress was halted. When I abruptly swung my head around to see what had snagged me, I saw that it was the kitten, which had planted itself firmly astride my tail and was now playing with the tail's tail end, which invariably tends to sway as if possessing a mind of its own.

"Stop that," I snapped, but the kitten seemed to enjoy the swishing movement so much it kept grabbing at my fluffy appendage.

"Max," said Odelia warningly.

"Stop that, please?" I asked.

But then the kitten suddenly dug its teeth into my tail and I screamed, "Yikes!"

"Max!" Odelia said. "Don't be rude!"

"But she just bit me in the tail!"

"She's just playing," she said, then picked up my little nemesis, and checked her. "So you think she's a she?"

"Of course she's a she. Don't you think a cat can tell whether another cat is a he or a she?"

"Don't be a smart-ass. Here," she said, planting the other two kittens in front of me. "Tell me what they are."

I scowled at the foul creatures, then pointed at the black one. "He," I said. Then pointed at the white one. "He."

"Thanks, Max," said Odelia, and picked up all three kittens. "Now for the most important part. What shall we name them? Any suggestions?"

She was rocking them in her arms now, even though they tried to squirm away.

My suggestion was Menace Number One, Menace Number Two and Menace Number Three, but something told me Odelia might not agree with my naming convention. So instead I said, "Why don't you ask Gran? She named the rest of us."

Odelia nodded. "Great idea. I'll ask her."

I didn't know if this was such a good idea, for Gran has a habit of picking names from the soaps she watches. I was named after Max Halloran, a doctor on *General Hospital* who was accused of fathering triplets with his mother's twin sister's mobster fiancé's younger sister's best friend. And Dooley could trace the origin of his name to a casting director on *The Bold and the Beautiful.* Harriet, on the other hand, was named after *Harriet the Spy,* apparently a book Odelia's mom had always liked.

Brutus, of course, had been named by Chase's mom, his

original owner. I have no idea what inspired her, but Brutus has always been a butch cat, so the name seemed apt.

The kittens, meanwhile, had managed to tumble back onto the kitchen counter, and were now digging their teeth into the carton box, ripping it into tiny pieces and spreading it across the floor like confetti.

I had to bite my tongue not to make a scathing remark about littering, but managed to restrain myself with a powerful effort. This was, after all, Odelia's house, and if she felt like raising a trio of hell-raisers, that was her prerogative.

I vowed, however, that the moment she turned her back I was going to do some serious schooling of my own. I like to run a tight ship when she's not around, and I intended to keep it that way.

CHAPTER 3

Odelia could have stayed with the little cuties all morning, but unfortunately she had to go to work. By then, Chase was up, his alarm clock having launched into a cheerful rendition of Pharrell Williams's *Happy*, and the hunky cop had woken up with a groan.

When she arrived at the top of the stairs, she was greeted by the pleasant scene of Chase sitting up in bed and stretching. The man was built like a tank, and even though she'd already seen him sans T-shirt many times since their first meeting, it was still a sight for sore eyes. Her eyes weren't sore now, though. Instead, they were sparkling.

"What's with the racket?" asked Chase now as she stepped into the bedroom and sat down on the edge of the bed to feast her eyes on the man's perfect physique from up close.

"Oh, just three kittens left in a box on my doorstep," she explained.

He did a double take. "Wait, what now?"

She nodded. "Yup. Someone left three kittens outside, with a note asking me to take care of them. Oh, Chase, you should see them. They're just the cutest little babies!"

"Kittens," he said, as if she'd just announced the world was ending. "Three of them."

"I would have brought them up but I didn't know if you were awake yet."

He was awake now, that much was obvious. Awake and not entirely happy about this turn of events. He squeezed his eyes shut then opened them again, as if hoping this had all been a bad dream. "So you're telling me you've decided to adopt three more cats?"

"I haven't adopted them," she specified. "Someone left them on my doorstep."

He laughed an incredulous laugh. "You're not seriously thinking about keeping them, are you?"

She experienced a slight diminution of the love and affection she felt for him from the moment he'd walked into her life. "I haven't decided yet. Why? Don't you like kittens?"

Chase hesitated. He could probably sense he'd just stepped on a potential landmine that was about to go off at the slightest provocation. Ever so carefully, he said, "You already have four cats. Three more makes seven. That's seven cats. Four plus three. Seven."

"Your grasp on basic math is astounding, Chase," she said. "Yes, seven cats, divided over two homes, makes three-and-a-half cats per home. I know people that have a dozen cats." She didn't add that she personally felt that a dozen cats was a little ambitious for any homeowner, even if they adored the furry creatures. She wanted to gauge Chase's response.

He blinked and gulped. "A dozen."

She nodded cheerfully. "A dozen cats. And a happy home it is, too."

"A dozen cats," he muttered, and started to shake his head. Then he paused mid-shake, and gave her an odd look. "Today isn't April Fool's, is it?"

Her lips tightened. "No, today isn't April Fool's. And I

don't understand what the big deal is. Seven cats is nothing. Besides, like I said, I haven't decided if I'm going to keep them or not." Though she was starting to lean towards adopting them if Chase kept this up.

"Think about it," he said, holding up an admonishing hand. "Think hard. I mean, there might be other families that want to adopt a cat. In fact there may be three families out there, extremely keen to adopt a cute little kitty and you hogging all three of them would put those families in a state of deep, profound sadness. Don't be a hogger, babe."

He had a point, of course. She couldn't very well hog all the cats in Hampton Cove. That simply wouldn't be fair.

And she would have discussed the ins and outs of cat adoption in more detail if Chase's phone hadn't developed suicidal tendencies and leaped from the nightstand when it started buzzing frantically. He picked it up and grunted, "It's your uncle," then answered by growling, "Yeah, Alec." He listened for a moment, then raised his eyes to Odelia, and nodded. "I'll be there in five." When he disconnected, he gave her a quizzical look. "Mh."

"What is it?" She knew that look. Something had happened. Something bad.

"It's Jeb Pott," he said, scratching his ear.

"The actor? What about him?"

"He's just been arrested."

"Arrested? What did he do this time? Joyriding? Drunk and disorderly?" The famous actor was, in spite of his age, still a bad boy personified, and had been wreaking havoc across town for the past couple of weeks now. If he wasn't speeding through downtown Hampton Cove, spooking senior citizens, he could be found passed out in the local park, having succumbed to an abundance of vodka or some other intoxicant, liquid or powdered.

But Chase was slowly shaking his head. "This time he's really done it."

"Don't keep me in suspense, Chase. What did he do?"

Jeb Pott was one of her favorite actors—possibly *the* favorite actor of every woman her age—and to watch him self-destruct had hurt and annoyed Odelia a great deal.

"He's murdered his ex-wife. Your uncle just found her body in his lodge, the knife in his bed, her blood on his hands."

CHAPTER 4

I'd joined Odelia as she drove out to the house where Jeb Pott lived, and so had Dooley, my best friend and part-time housemate. Chase had taken his own pickup and was leading the way, with Odelia following close behind.

"So who is this Jeb Pott?" asked Dooley now.

"He's a world-famous actor," said Odelia.

She looked unhappy at this turn of events, and I didn't wonder. She loves Jeb Pott and has seen every picture the man has ever made, from his humble arthouse movie beginnings to his blockbuster turn as swashbuckler in the remake of *Captain Blood*. The man isn't merely a star. He's a mega-star. Or at least was, until his recent disastrous divorce.

"We've seen him, remember, Dooley?" I said. "He played Captain Blood in *Captain Blood*. They call him the new Errol Flynn."

"Oh, right," said Dooley, though it was obvious he had no idea what I was talking about. The sight of three kittens cavorting about our living room had startled Dooley as much as it had me, and this had shortened his attention span which now made him tune out to some extent. Dooley's mind is such that it can only hold two ideas at the same time, and right now it was overrun with images of kittens dangling from the curtains, swinging from the ceiling lights, cavorting on the kitchen counter, and peeing in Odelia's flowerpots.

"I like him," said Odelia. "I like him a lot. I think he's one of the most talented actors of his generation, or any generation, for that matter. He's always been one of my favorites, until..." She dug her teeth into her lower lip.

"Until the divorce," I said in a low voice.

She nodded and gripped her steering wheel a little tighter. "Until the divorce," she said quietly.

Jeb Pott's career could be divided into two distinct periods: the slow rise to the absolute pinnacle of fame and glory, and his post-divorce period, when his star power had begun to wane and he'd gone from hero to zero in the space of a few short weeks.

His ex-wife Camilla Kirby had filed for divorce on the grounds of domestic violence, cruelty and substance abuse and had shown the proof by parading in front of the world media with a big purple bruise on her cheek, the result of an encounter with Jeb's fist.

Jeb had claimed foul play and said she'd made up both bruise and abuse, but by then it was too late, the actor's reputation irreparably damaged, and turned into a pariah by the same Tinseltown that had hailed him as its most popular star only a few short weeks before.

"Oh, how fickle fame is," I said softly.

"So what happened to this Jeb Pott?" asked Dooley.

"He allegedly beat his wife, and now he allegedly murdered her," I said.

"Nothing alleged about it," said Odelia. "Camille Kirby is dead and Jeb was practically covered in her blood, the murder weapon lying next to him on the bed, his prints all over it." She was shaking her head. "I find this very hard to believe. How could he..." Her voice caught and she haltingly said, in a strange, wobbly tone, "I took his side, you know. In the divorce circus? I thought she was lying. And now this."

I shook my head sadly. Human drama. It never fails to grip. It's just so much more poignant than feline drama, don't you think? Just look at all the soap operas. Or have you ever seen a soap about cats pulling each other's hair? Then again, cats don't often buy soap, so daytime TV doesn't have that much of an incentive to target them as their audience.

Chase's pickup pulled off the road and stopped in front of a wooden gate. A cop was parked in front of it, and when he saw Chase he held up his hand in greeting and used a button on a keypad next to the gate. He spoke into the intercom and the gate swung open.

Outside the gate, a dozen news vans were parked, with two dozen reporters, camera crew and photographers trying to catch a glimpse of what was happening beyond that gate.

When we arrived and were waved through, they started snapping pictures of Odelia and Chase and even me and Dooley. I grinned. "There are going to be a lot of editors in a lot of newsrooms across the country wondering what two cats are doing visiting the crime scene of one of the world's most famous actors."

"They're probably also wondering why I'm the only reporter allowed to enter the place," said Odelia, who didn't seem to enjoy being photographed by her colleagues as much as I'd expected. Then again, Odelia is not used to being at the center of attention. Usually she's the one out there, snapping pictures of the stars driving by in their limos.

"At least you didn't bring the kittens along," said Dooley, harping on the same theme that had occupied his mind from the moment we'd left the house.

"They're too young to travel," said Odelia absentmindedly

as she slipped her car into a parking spot, then unfastened her seatbelt and turned to us. "So you know what to do, right?"

"Relax," I said. "We're old paws at this by now."

"Old paws," said Dooley, chuckling. "Funny."

Odelia smiled. "Great. Go get them, boys."

Our task, if we chose to accept it, which we did, was to gather background information, and talk to any creature that might have seen something, heard something, sniffed something, or generally had information and a unique perspective to impart. It provided Odelia with those telling details that made her stories so vivid and unique.

So we set off in the direction of the lodge that was the hub of activity, crime scene people and cops buzzing about like so many flies, and vowed to make Odelia proud.

CHAPTER 5

It was with a heavy heart that Odelia took out her notebook. Normally she loved reporting on crime and spinning an entertaining yarn for her readers, but this particular case had struck close to home. She'd been a fan of Jeb's for as long as she could remember, and this murder suddenly painted her hero in a very unfavorable light indeed. Could it be that Jeb wasn't the quirky, talented actor she'd come to adore but a murdering psychopath instead?

Uncle Alec came walking out of the small lodge. He looked stricken, and held up a meaty paw when he saw her. "Better don't go in there, honey. It's not a pretty sight."

She nodded. "Where is Jeb?"

"We took him away already. He's cooling his heels in the lockup."

"Are you sure he did it?" she asked. It was the question that had been at the forefront of her mind ever since Chase had delivered the shocking news.

"No doubt about it," her uncle grumbled with a sad look on his hangdog face. At fifty-four, Alec Lip's face displayed the mileage he'd racked up as the town's chief of police and then some. His wispy gray hair was plastered to his skull as usual, and he hadn't shaved yet, probably having been called out of bed and having driven straight there.

"And is it... Camilla Kirby?"

He nodded dourly. "No doubt about that, either. She has so many stab wounds it looks like Jeb must have been in a murderous frenzy." He shook his head again. "Terrible business. Just terrible," he muttered.

"Maybe someone else did it and is trying to put the blame on Jeb?"

Her uncle gave her a skeptical look. "The knife was right next to him on the bed, his prints all over it. Her blood on his hands and clothes. Almost as if he'd been bathing in it. We even found her blood in his ears. I'm sorry, honey, but Jeb Pott is guilty as hell."

"But what was Camilla doing out here? I thought they were divorced."

"They were. All we know for certain right now is that she took a flight out here from LA late last night, then took a taxi here. She arrived at exactly…" He took out his notebook. "Three forty-five."

"Middle of the night."

"Uh-huh. The taxi driver told me he warned her about getting out of his cab in the middle of the night in the middle of nowhere but she was unconcerned. Giddy, even, according to his statement. As if she couldn't wait to meet…"

"Jeb," said Odelia quietly. "So who else lives here?"

"Place belongs to Jeb's other ex-wife. Helena Grace. She's lived here with their daughter Fae for the past fifteen years."

"It's the house Jeb bought when he and Helena moved here from Rome."

"Is that right?" said Uncle Alec, looking amused at being upstaged.

"Jeb and Helena met twenty-five years ago in Italy. He

was filming a movie out there and she had a small part. She played his nurse, tasked with nursing him back to health after his fighter jet was shot down by the Germans. It was a World War II drama."

"Right," he said. "Anyway, the front gate can only be opened either from the main house, where Helena and her daughter live, or from the lodge, where Jeb was staying."

"So Camilla arrived at the gate, Jeb let her in and..."

"Killed her, yeah. Must have happened soon after she arrived. Abe puts time of death around four o'clock."

"Who called it in?" she asked as she surveyed the frenzied scene. A stretcher was now being carried out, and she turned away her head. She might be there to report on a crime but that didn't mean she reveled in this kind of death and mayhem. She could write a good article without mentioning all the gore other reporters seemed to salivate over.

"That's the weirdest thing," said Uncle Alec, scratching his scalp with his pencil. "Anonymous phone call. Neighbor walking his dog at the time of the murder. Said he heard a scream and took a closer look. Said he saw a man attacking a woman. So he called it in."

"No idea who the witness is?"

"No idea. Which isn't unusual," he hastened to say when he saw her skeptical expression. "Some people just don't want to get involved in anything to do with the police."

"So he actually saw the murder—actually saw Jeb murder his ex-wife?"

"Uh-huh." He groped around for his reading glasses. "Where are the darn things?" he grumbled. Odelia plucked them from the top of his head where he'd just put them and he gave her a grateful grin. "Thanks, hon." He frowned at his notes. "Here it is. Caller said he heard a woman scream bloody murder. Said a man who looked like Jeb Pott attacked her."

"So there's a witness to the murder," she said, deflating. She'd hoped against hope that Jeb was innocent, but it was becoming more and more obvious that he was guilty.

"I'd be more satisfied if I could talk to this witness, of course," said Uncle Alec. "But with all the evidence we have right now there's no doubt Jeb Pott will be convicted of murdering his ex-wife in cold blood." He lowered his voice. "We also found a ton of cocaine in the house, along with at least a dozen other illegal substances and crates full of hard liquor and booze. If all this stuff shows up on Jeb's tox screen the guy was high as a kite when he did what he did. Maybe he didn't even realize what he was doing."

Odelia nodded. More proof that the stories of Jeb's substance abuse were true.

"Honestly, Odelia, this is a guy who went all Charles Manson on that poor woman. She never stood a chance. The moment she walked into this lodge she was a dead woman."

CHAPTER 6

Dooley and I idly inspected the terrain that surrounded the lodge. It mainly consisted of ferns, wild geraniums and different types of grasses. It all looked very inviting for a nap.

"I don't like it, Max," said Dooley, using one of his favorite phrases.

"I don't like it either," I intimated. "This Jeb guy is a terrific actor. I thought he was great in *Captain Blood* and those westerns. I never get tired of watching his movies."

"I don't mean Jeb," said Dooley. "It's the kittens. I don't think I like them very much."

"Which is only natural," I assured him. "Nobody likes kittens, Dooley. Except humans, of course."

"Odelia likes them."

"Case in point. That's because kittens have a tendency to play on humans' heartstrings. They tug those strings so hard they leave those poor humans giddy with affection and a distinct sense of dubious attachment to the furry little creatures."

"They're very rude," said Dooley. "And they don't respect us older cats."

"No, they don't."

Even before we'd left the house to go on this fact-finding mission with Odelia, the threesome had used my water bowl to dunk a paper ball into and had emptied out my bowl of Cat Snax. And when Odelia had refilled my bowl, and had placed three smaller bowls, one for each kitten, they'd finished their own bowls then mine in one fell swoop!

"No respect at all," I agreed with my buddy.

"They're taking over the house, Max. They're even peeing in the corners, marking off their territory—our territory!"

"I know," I sighed. "But what can we do? Odelia loves them to death—even though she only met them this morning."

"We need to teach them some manners, Max. Teach them to respect their elders."

"I know, but Odelia strictly forbade me to do exactly that."

"But we can't just let them walk all over us!" he cried, indicating just how riled up he was. Dooley is usually a very peaceable cat, and this proved how he was being pushed to the brink and beyond by our unexpected guests, just like I was. "Maybe we should send in Brutus to deal with the three little brutes," Dooley said now. "Or Harriet—or both!"

I gave this some thought. There was no doubt Dooley had made a valid point. Neither Harriet or Brutus had been cautioned by Odelia. Yet. So they were officially in the clear, able to admonish to their heart's content. And frankly speaking Brutus could be very severe if he wanted to be, and so could Harriet. If I were a kitten and I saw Harriet or Brutus coming—or both—I'd be afraid. I'd be very, very afraid.

Bucked up by these uplifting thoughts, I discovered we'd

reached the back of the small lodge. A pile of discarded and empty glass bottles was lying there, testament to the preference for alcoholic beverages of the lodge's current occupant. Beyond the pile of bottles an ashtray rested on a bench, overflowing with weirdly shaped cigarette butts.

"Why do humans smoke and drink so much, Max?" asked Dooley.

"Beats me," I said.

"They possess a tendency towards self-destruction, don't they?"

"You can say that again."

"They possess a tendency towards self-destruction, don't they?"

"I didn't mean literally repeat—oh, never mind," I said. I'd spotted a tiny birdie sitting and singing in a nearby tree and padded over to take a closer look at this fluffy little friend.

On the whole, the relationship between cats and birds is fraught with a certain tension. Birds, as a rule, don't like cats. Probably because cats, as a species, tend to eat birds. Not that I'm one of those cats, per se. Odelia taught us a long time ago that sometimes we need to sink the savage feline into the civilized feline, and has strictly forbidden us from ever taking a feathered life.

"Yoo-hoo, birdie," I said now.

The bird glanced down in our direction, did a visible double take, blanched to the root of its downy gray feathers, and fluttered off as fast as its tiny wings could carry it.

"Too bad," I said.

"What is, Max?"

"That birds take this instant dislike to us just because we're cats."

"It's anti-cat bias," Dooley agreed.

As far as I could tell, no other feathered creatures were anywhere nearby, and I was about to give up this fact-finding mission as a dud when I saw that a young woman came walking in our direction through a small patch of gray birch trees. There was a path there that led straight from the house to this lodge, and she was bouncing down it at a brisk pace. She vaguely resembled Jeb, and I wondered if she was in any way related to the actor.

When she came upon us, she smiled prettily. "Oh, hey, you two cuties. I've never seen you here before." She crouched down next to us, and tickled me behind the ear, then rubbed Dooley's head, then scratched me under the chin. In response, we both closed our eyes and started purring up a storm. Now here was a human to whom I took an instant shine. Pro-human bias, I guess. And we were still purring when Odelia rounded the lodge and came into view. When she saw us fraternizing with another human, she smiled.

"I see you've met my cats."

"Oh, are these two sweeties yours? They're so cute!" the girl said. Then she seemed to sober and rose to her feet. "You're Odelia Poole, aren't you?"

Odelia seemed surprised to be recognized. "Yes, I am. Have we met?"

"Not in person. I love your articles for the Gazette, and I've seen your picture." She glanced around. "Um, I need to ask you a favor, Miss Poole."

"Odelia. And you are…"

"Oh, sorry. How rude of me." The girl thrust out a slender hand that was attached to a slim arm, which was connected to a willowy body. "My name is Fae. I'm Jeb's daughter."

"Oh, of course," said Odelia, shaking the girl's hand.

She was probably all of seventeen, or maybe even sixteen, and looked very young and very pretty. Striking large eyes and a pale heart-shaped face with high cheekbones.

"I know what you must be thinking," said Fae. "My father

did the most unspeakable thing. But I can assure you that he didn't do what they're accusing him of, Odelia."

"He didn't?"

The girl shook her head decidedly. "My daddy would never murder anyone. He couldn't hurt a fly." She took a deep breath. "Which is why I want you to find out who's framing him for murder. I want you to find out and then I want you to tell the police who the real murderer is." She took out her wallet before Odelia could reply, and pressed a small wad of green bills into her hand. "Consider this an advance for future services rendered. I'll pay you whatever you want, but please, Miss Poole," she said, and clasped Odelia's arm, fixing her with a pleading look. "Please please please clear my father's name?"

CHAPTER 7

Odelia didn't know what to say. "I don't know if…" she began.

"Oh, I know you're not a private detective—not a licensed one, anyway. But I also know that you've helped the police solve countless murders, and that you're very good at what you do. If there's one person who can clear my daddy's name it's you, Miss Poo—I mean Odelia. So please, please, please, please, please take me on as your client?"

"Like you said, I'm not a detective, Fae," said Odelia. "I'm a reporter, so…"

"But you *have* to find out what really happened. You just *have* to. My daddy—he *can't* be in jail. He's not going to last a week—even a day. He's a sensitive soul—a poet and a tender-hearted man. He simply won't *survive* if he's locked up in that dreadful place."

Odelia remembered her uncle's description of the murder scene and thought that Jeb Pott was anything but a tender-hearted soul. More like a crazed killer.

"Fae, even if I wanted to, I don't have the skillset to—"

"Oh, but you do! I've read all your articles, and I've heard all the stories. Mom says you're an ace detective and you're the one who's solved all those murders, not the police—and definitely not your uncle. You and only you have been solving crime in this town."

"I'm sure that's not true," said Odelia. "The thing is, to do what you're asking me to do—to investigate Camilla Kirby's murder, and to take you on as a client…" She hesitated.

A look of distress had crossed the girl's face. It was obvious she wasn't going to take no for an answer.

Odelia decided just to say it. "I'm not entirely convinced your father is innocent, Fae."

The girl had gripped Odelia's arm again. She had a firm grasp, in spite of her thin frame. So thin Odelia thought she might be a model. She remembered reading something about Jeb launching her in that industry when she was fifteen. Or she could be confusing her with another celebrity's daughter. "Oh, but I'll convince you. Why do you think he did it?"

"Well, for one thing, he's the only one out here—staying in this lodge. No traces have been found of anyone else inside the cabin."

"The killer could have worn rubber-soled shoes and have entered the cabin while my daddy was asleep."

"Yes, but that doesn't explain why Camilla's blood is all over your father's clothes, and why the knife is covered in his fingerprints." She decided to neglect to mention the part about blood in Jeb's ear, where it must have splattered when he murdered his ex-wife.

"The killer could easily have smeared that blood on Daddy while he was asleep, and planted the knife in his bed," she insisted stubbornly.

All true, Odelia agreed, and was surprised to find the girl's thoughts following her own so closely. "But there's a witness, Fae. A witness who saw what happened."

"A witness?" The girl frowned.

"Yes, this witness saw your father arguing with Camilla and then attacking her. He's the one who called the police. He's the reason they showed up here so fast and were able to arrest your father." Before he could get rid of the body and cover his tracks.

"So who is this witness? Have the police told you his name?"

"They don't know his name. He doesn't want to come forward. The only thing we know about him is that he was walking his dog."

"Here? Inside the gate?"

"Out on the street."

The girl laughed. "Oh, but don't you see?! He's lying! There's no way you can look in from the street. There's the fence, and it's overgrown with weeds and whatever. So this witness must be the real killer—he's the one trying to blame this whole thing on Daddy!"

"I don't know…" said Odelia, wishing those reporters would take a hike so she could take a look at that fence herself. Fae had a point. How could this witness have looked through the lodge's window if the entire place was fenced off?

Fae clasped Odelia's hands in hers. "Oh, won't you help me? My daddy is innocent. Absolutely innocent. He didn't kill Camilla. I'm one hundred percent sure he didn't."

Odelia studied Jeb's daughter, who stood looking at her with a pleading expression on her face, practically willing her to take the case. But she decided she simply couldn't. So she handed back the cash. "I'm so sorry, Fae, but I can't. Like I said, I'm not a detective."

A mutinous look came over the girl's face. It was obvious she was used to getting what she wanted.

"You don't believe me, do you? You think I'm just a silly little girl who loves her daddy so much she'd do anything to save him—even if he's guilty of murder. But I'm not. I'm not an innocent little girl. I know what's out there in the world. I've seen evil and I know what it looks like. I'm a model, you see, and I've come across my fair share of predators and monsters in this business. I've looked into their eyes and seen the depravity and the horror and the lechery. And I've looked into my father's eyes and seen nothing but love and tenderness and kindness. He's a true innocent, and that's why he finds it so hard to live in this world sometimes. People can be cruel, Odelia. Very, very cruel." And with these words, she abruptly turned on her heel and strode off back in the direction of the manor house.

"That was tough," said Max, who hadn't spoken a word throughout the exchange.

"Yeah, very tough," Odelia agreed. "But I can't take Fae's money. She wants me to prove her father's innocence, and I can't. Because he did it, Max. Jeb Pott is a murderer. He's a brutal cold-hearted killer and I'm not going to try and prove otherwise."

CHAPTER 8

Frankly I didn't see what else there was for us to do out there. We'd tried to talk to a potential witness, who'd taken flight the moment he or she laid eyes on us, and now we were simply cooling our heels wasting time while the kittens were probably tearing the house apart back home. But Odelia was still snooping around, and I didn't feel like pawing it all the way home, instead opting to wait until Odelia was finished and gave us a lift.

And since we were out there anyway, with nothing to do, we decided to take a turn around the grounds and take in the scenery. To be absolutely honest I also wanted to take a closer look at that ginormous mansion at the end of the driveway. It is my experience, borne out by years of associating with humans, that people who own mansions often have pets, and those pets are more often than not pampered little creatures who enjoy the very best in gourmet food that money can buy. And since I was getting a little peckish—not to mention that the kittens had stolen my food—I thought it was only fair to take a peek and maybe even a bite in yonder pet haven.

And so wander yonder we did, and soon found ourselves rounding the house and looking for a way into the kitchen, where, once again according to my extensive experience, often cat food can be found—or even dog food. At that juncture it didn't do to be picky.

The deck rose into view and we moved over to check it out. And that's when we found the same girl who'd approached Odelia with her incredible proposition, crying her heart out. She wasn't crying in little sobs either but in big gulping gulps, wailing away.

"Poor girl," said Dooley.

"Yeah. It's not her fault her dad is a homicidal maniac who murders women for fun."

"Maybe Odelia should have taken on her case?"

"Maybe. Though from what I can gather he's guilty, Dooley. And it's very hard to prove that a guilty man didn't do it. Nor should Odelia even have to try. Guilty people belong in jail." That's what Odelia has always taught us and it's what I truly believe.

"Do you think Fae wants Odelia to prove that her dad didn't do it even if he did?"

"Looked that way to me. She just wants her daddy back, whether he's guilty or not."

We both glanced up at the teenager, who still sat there heaving big wailing gulps of breath, from time to time pausing to blow her nose in a stack of Kleenex she kept on hand.

A woman who slightly resembled Fae came walking out of the house and placed her arm around the young woman's shoulder. "It's all right, honey. Everything will be all right."

"No, it won't, Mom!" the girl cried, shaking off her mother's arm. "Things will never be all right again. Never ever ever!"

And then she practically leaped into the house, leaving

her mother looking distraught and worried. The mom picked up a tissue for herself and blew her nose. Her eyes were red-rimmed and she looked like she'd been crying herself.

"This man has broken so many hearts," said Dooley, shaking his head.

A little fluffy doggie came tripping out of the house. The moment it saw us it stood there, panting slightly, vibrating on its tiny paws, as if it had never seen a pair of cats before.

"Hey there, dog," I said, hoping it wouldn't start barking and acting mad like most dogs do when they come across a cat.

It gave one sharp bark and Fae's mother looked up. When she saw us, she smiled. "What are you sweethearts doing here?" She came over and crouched down next to us. "You look like you belong to someone," she said, gently stroking my fur. "You're too nice-looking and well-groomed to be feral cats."

I did the purring thing again, and so did Dooley when the woman extended the same courtesy to him.

The doggie had cocked its head in our direction and stood staring with a strange look on its face. It probably wasn't used to seeing his human engage with a pair of cats.

"You know, Max," said Dooley now as he cast a glance at the pile of tissues on the table. "Maybe we have to convince Odelia to take on this case anyway."

"I'm starting to think so, too," I said as the woman suddenly burst into tears and some of those tears splashed across my head like the dewy rain.

I sneezed and she cried some more.

"She's clearly heart-broken and so is her daughter," said Dooley. "I don't think humans would cry so much over a man if that man was a murderous maniacal monster."

"You're right," I said. The plight of these women touched

my heart. And so did the bowl of food Fae's mom pushed in our direction and from which I was taking hearty bites.

So we're cats. We fall in love with any human that feeds us.

The woman finally disappeared into the house, presumably to look for her daughter, and then it was just us and the dog, whom I'd identified as a Bichon Frisé dog, one of those hairy white creatures that look like a walking ball of fluff.

"What do you think, dog?" I asked around a mouth filled with kibble.

"You do know that's my food you're eating, right?" said the dog, head still cocked and giving us sour looks.

"And very tasty it is, too," said Dooley. "Thank you, dog."

"The name is Sasha, and I'd say you're welcome if I'd had a choice in the matter. As it is, my human seems to like you, so I will not bite you in the ankles. I repeat, I will not bite you in the ankles."

"Very kind of you," I said.

"I probably should, though," said Sasha, indicating we were not in the clear yet. So I took a few quick bites, just in case she changed her mind and went for my ankles anyway. Although, do cats even have ankles? "It's in the dog rulebook, you know," Sasha continued.

"What is?" I asked.

"When confronted with an invading feline, go for the ankles. Printed right there in black and white."

"Right," I said. Of all the dogs in the world, we had to come across a fanatic and a rule follower. "So what can you tell us about Jeb Pott and the woman he murdered?"

"Yes, do you believe Jeb did it or that he was framed, like Fae seems to think?" Dooley added.

"I like Jeb," said Sasha. "He's a decent human being. He once took me to New Zealand on a trip. Only I got kicked out by some politician on account of the fact that I'd neglected to bring along my passport." She shrugged. "Humans. They're just weird."

"Tell us about it," said Dooley.

At least we agreed on one thing.

"So no, if I'm absolutely honest, I don't think Jeb could ever murder Camilla."

"Wait, you knew Camilla?" I asked.

"Sure. I was hers and Jeb's when they were married. But after the divorce there was so much lawyerly fuss that Jeb decided to give me to Helena and Fae, so here I am."

"What about Camilla? Didn't she want you?"

"Not sure, actually. There was some legal wrangling, and the lawyers decided that nothing was decided until everything was decided. About the divorce, I mean. And by then I'd become so accustomed to living here that I'm actually happy nothing was decided."

It all sounded pretty complicated, and I could tell from the strange look on Dooley's face he had a hard time following the story, too. But regardless, one thing clearly stood out: here sat yet another individual who was familiar with Jeb and believed he was innocent.

"But then how do you explain what happened?" I asked.

Sasha shrugged. "I can't. In case you hadn't noticed, I'm a lapdog, not a member of a K9 unit. But what I can tell you is that Jeb had a lot of enemies, and I wouldn't put it past them to pull a dirty trick like this on him."

"Or on Camilla," I said. After all, she was the one who was dead right now.

"Or Camilla," agreed Sasha.

I shared a meaningful look with Dooley. "I think we need to have a long talk with our human, Dooley," I said.

"I think so, too," he agreed.

And then we took some more kibble. What? My mother always taught me never to skip a free meal. And I'm nothing if not a momma's cat.

CHAPTER 9

Odelia was in her office, typing up her piece on the Camilla Kirby murder, when her boss walked in. Dan Goory, a white-bearded pint-sized man, had been running the Hampton Cove Gazette for so long now people identified him with it. He'd started the paper back in the stone age, and had kept it running all this time, single-handedly writing most of the copy, until he'd started looking for someone to help him lighten his load, and had found, after a lot of trial and error, the right person in Odelia. Her predecessors hadn't fared as well as she had, but their amicable collaboration had been so successful that there was even talk now of her taking over the paper if or when Dan would finally decide to retire.

She hoped that day would never come, for she knew that running a paper was a different beast from filling its pages with newsworthy stories. As it was, Dan took care of the business side as well as the editing and she was free to write articles people enjoyed to read.

"So Jeb Pott, huh?" said Dan now, in his low gravelly voice, courtesy of smoking a pack a day for years, even though he'd now stopped—doctor's orders. "Who would have thunk?"

"Not me," said Odelia, raising her hands from the keyboard and lacing her fingers behind her head. "In fact I was more than a little shocked to hear it."

"Yeah, me too," Dan admitted. "Even though Pott is an amateur compared to greats like Olivier and Gielgud."

"Who?" said Odelia with a slight grin.

"Oh, you barbarian." He paused, flicking an imaginary speck of dust from his sleeve. Today he'd opted for a heliotrope shirt with yellow suspenders, and looked very snazzy. "So what do you reckon? Did he do it?"

"Looks like," said Odelia. "At least that's what the police think."

"We both know the police aren't always right."

"We do know that, but this time I think they are." She ticked off the items on her fingers. "A witness saw the murder—actually witnessed the murder and called it in. Camilla's blood was all over Jeb, and his prints all over the knife. And he'd invited her to come visit."

"But why? What was he hoping to accomplish?"

"As far as Uncle Alec could tell from the text messages on her phone he was looking for a reconciliation. He said he still loved her and couldn't stop thinking about her in spite of the divorce, and he wanted to try and heal the rift and put the past behind them."

"And apparently she felt the same way or else she wouldn't have flown all the way out here to see him."

"Apparently."

They were both silent for a beat, then Dan rapped the door with his knuckle and said, "Keep up the good work, Poole, and write me a killer article, will you? I have a feeling this might be our biggest issue yet."

"Will do, sir," she said dutifully, and bent over her laptop to pound out the rest of her article. She looked up when the outer door to the office swung open and the bell jangled.

"Where is my granddaughter?" a familiar voice rasped. "I demand to see my granddaughter!"

"In here, Gran!" she yelled.

Her grandmother came striding into the office. She was out of breath, and had twin circles of crimson dotting her cheeks. The elderly woman was wearing her large-framed glasses, had her hair done up in tiny white curls, and as usual looked the spitting image of a sweet old lady, ready to dole out candy to kids. In actual fact she was anything but sweet. Vesta Muffin could be pretty caustic if she wanted to be, and she often wanted to be.

"What's all this nonsense about you going out on a case and not inviting me along?" she demanded, planting her fists on Odelia's desk and leaning over so far her head was almost touching her granddaughter's.

"I didn't know you worked here," Odelia quipped, but Gran wasn't having any of it.

"You know as well as I do that a true flogger, in order to be successful, needs to upload fresh content all the time." She tapped the desk impatiently. "I need you to let me in on this case, Odelia. I've lost so many followers over this Yellow Parka MacGyver Gang fiasco it's not pretty. I need a big hit —pronto!"

"Don't you mean vlogging?"

"That's what I said. Flogging. I need this, Odelia. I need this bad."

"You sound just like my boss," said Odelia. But Gran was eyeing her so intently she quickly relented. "All right, all right, you can tag along. But there's no case this time, Gran. Just a murder to cover for the paper."

"What do you mean there's no case? A woman was murdered, right?"

"Yes, she was, but Alec already caught the killer."

"So fast? That's impossible!"

"It was Jeb Pott. He was caught practically red-handed. Literally, actually."

"Oh, darn it. I liked that kid."

Odelia refrained from mentioning that that kid was a fifty-five-year-old man. Instead, she said, "So you see? There is no case. No murder to solve. No killer to catch."

Gran plunked down on the chair opposite hers. "At least let me interview Jeb Pott. Big star like him—my follower count will shoot through the roof."

"What do you care how many followers you have?" Odelia asked. She didn't understand this obsession with followers. At all.

"I need to beat Scarlett Canyon," Gran said, looking grim now. "That jerk has started flogging, too, and she's got more followers in one week than me in a month."

"She's also fighting crime now?" asked Odelia, wondering when this enmity between her grandmother and Scarlett Canyon would finally be over. All of Hampton Cove would sleep more easily when it was.

"She's giving beauty tips," said Gran, frowning darkly. "Which in her case means sitting in front of a camera wriggling her cleavage and pretending to know something about cosmetics. Next thing I know she'll be doing a striptease act. Anything to get more followers." Catching Odelia's inquisitive look, she added, "The more followers you have the more chances of landing one of those lucrative influencer deals. L'Oréal or Lancôme will pay big bucks to push their products on the channels of people with lots and lots of followers."

"They won't be pushing L'Oréal on a YouTube channel about murder."

"Of course not, silly. But then Scarlett isn't on YouTube.

She's on Instagram. But it's the thought that counts. I can't let her best me, so I need more followers. Otherwise she'll never let me live it down."

Scarlett Canyon and Gran had been mortal enemies ever since Gran caught her doing the horizontal mambo on her kitchen table with Grandpa Jack. Things had gone from bad to worse ever since, especially since Scarlett had been Gran's best friend before the incident.

"So are you going to let me interview Jeb Pott or not?" Gran insisted.

"I don't even know if *I'll* be able to interview Jeb. Uncle Alec gives me a lot of leeway but he draws the line at actually jeopardizing a conviction. But I'll see what I can do," she added when Gran pulled one of her unhappy faces.

Gran got up and patted her cheek. "Good girl. And if you stumble across another dead body, this time let me know, all right? I need all the flogging I can get."

And after uttering these immortal words, she strode back out of the office.

CHAPTER 10

Peace had finally returned to the office and only the sounds of fingers tapping keyboards could be heard as Odelia and Dan worked silently in adjacent offices, hard at work to put out a killer edition of the Gazette. When Odelia's phone rang, she started and almost knocked over her cup of coffee.

"Yes, Uncle, what is it?" she asked when she saw it was him.

"I thought you'd want to know that Jeb denies the charges. Or rather, he's denying being aware that he killed his ex-wife."

"You mean he doesn't remember?"

"He says he passed out and doesn't remember a thing. He's pretty sure he would never kill his wife, though. As if that means a thing in his current situation."

"Is that even possible? To murder a person and not remember?"

"Judging from the copious amounts of narcotics and alcohol he had in his system that's certainly a possibility, although the coroner reckons that it would have been pretty hard for him to murder anyone in his condition. Passed out sounds about right. In fact it's a minor miracle he didn't kill himself, instead of Camilla."

"So what are you saying? That he didn't kill her?"

"Well, Abe reckons that a man who's been abusing intoxicants on such a scale could probably still function where others would have succumbed, so there's that to consider."

"Uh-huh," she said, frowning as she took in this new information. "Okay. So this doesn't change anything, right?"

"No, it doesn't." He noisily cleared his throat. "There's something else."

"What?"

"Camilla received a bunch of texts inviting her to Hampton Cove, right?"

"The texts that said he still loved her, wanted to reconcile, yadda yadda yadda."

"Chase did a routine check of Jeb's phone and didn't find a trace of those texts."

"Weird."

"Not so weird. He could have used a second phone."

"And did he?"

"Now this is where it does get weird. Those texts were sent from a burner phone."

"Why would Jeb use a burner phone?"

"It gets weirder: there's no trace of that phone. We searched his lodge top to bottom. Nothing."

"Jeb could have sent those texts and then dumped the phone."

"But why would he do that? And why not send his wife a text from his own phone?"

"Maybe.... he wanted to keep it a secret?"

"That doesn't make sense. He had no way of knowing how she'd react. She could have shown his messages to her lawyers. She could have contacted a reporter, heck she could have told the whole world. So why a burner phone? And why hide it?"

"You said it yourself. To deny that he sent them in case she reacted badly?"

"Maybe." He hesitated.

"Spill it. You know you want to tell me."

"That guy who called 911?"

"What about him?"

"We tried to trace him through his cell phone."

"And?"

"Dead end. Another burner phone. Now why would a neighbor walking his dog use a burner phone?"

That was a very good question, and one to which she didn't have an answer.

"Anyway, just thought you'd like to know. In case, uh, you decided to investigate further, I mean."

"Do you want me to investigate this further?"

"I'm not saying you should."

"So what are you saying, exactly?"

He sighed, and she could just imagine him sitting behind his desk, looking at his wilted office plants, and patting his wilted hair. "What I'm saying is that if you do investigate, I'm not going to stop you."

"Gotcha. What does Chase think?"

"Oh, he's happy as a clam that for once he doesn't have to chase witnesses and suspects and dig up clues."

"He thinks Jeb did it."

"Honey, everybody thinks Jeb did it. But just in case he didn't..."

"You want me to check so you can tie up those annoying loose ends."

"I hate loose ends, don't you?"

"Yes, I do," she said with a smile. "Look, Gran is dying to

interview Jeb. Do you think you can get us in the room with him?"

"Vesta and Jeb? No way!"

"I promise I'll make her behave."

"That's an empty promise and you know it. Besides, if the judge finds out I allowed my mother to interview my one and only suspect, there will be hell to pay."

"Or I could let her run this entire investigation all by herself. She's getting very good at it, and you know she's going to be the vlogging sensation of the year."

"And now you're blackmailing me."

"No, I'm not!"

"All right! Five minutes, and if she so much as puts one foot out of line, I'll yank her out of there so quick her dentures will rattle."

"Deal," she said, and disconnected just as the doorbell jangled again, and she watched Max and Dooley tiptoe into the office.

"Odelia!" Max said as he came tripping up to her desk, then hopped on top of it. "You have to accept Fae's offer. You just have to!"

"Oh... kay," she said. "What brought this on all of a sudden?"

"Fae and her mother were crying and crying and crying," said Dooley. "You can't believe how sad they are that Jeb is in jail now."

"And they have a little doggie, too," Max said. "The Bichon Frisé that used to belong to Jeb and Camilla? Her name is Sasha and she says Jeb would never hurt anyone. No way. So you see, Fae is right. Someone is trying to frame her daddy for murder, and you have to find out who the real killer is so Jeb can come home and be with his family again."

"Technically Helena is not his family anymore," said Odelia. "They're divorced."

"But Fae is still his daughter, and Sasha is still his dog—at least partly."

"Yes, they are," she admitted. She clapped her hands. "Well, isn't this your lucky day? It just so happens that Uncle Alec found some irregularities that indicate this story isn't as clear-cut as we've been led to believe. So he's asked me to look into the matter."

"So you think Jeb is innocent?" Dooley asked, his little face lighting up.

"No, I don't, but there are some things that need to be clarified."

Max gave her phone a little shove in her direction. "Call Fae. Tell her you'll take the case. Pretty please?"

"You should have seen how hard she was crying," said Dooley.

"Yeah," Max added, "she used so many paper tissues trees are crying, too."

Odelia laughed. "All right. I'll take the case."

She'd always trusted her cats' instincts. And if they thought that something funny was going on, and so did Uncle Alec, something funny definitely was going on.

CHAPTER 11

We were finally back at the house. I love prancing around and helping Odelia ferret out clues but you know what I love even more? To be home and lie on my favorite spot on my favorite couch. And having access to my food bowl and my litter box. So it was with a sinking heart that I discovered that not only had the kittens emptied out my food bowl again, but they'd also been playing in my litter box, spreading litter all over the kitchen floor.

Ugh.

"You guys!" I cried. "Why did you make such a mess?"

The three kittens sat next to one another and stared at me, then giggled and attacked me! One jumped on top of my head, another assaulted my tail, and the third one hopped onto my back and dug his tiny claws in!

"Ouch! Hey! What the…"

I tried to shake them off, but they were pretty tenacious.

"I'm the prime resident of this house and you're going to treat me with resp—ow!"

The one attached to my tail had sunk its teeth into this tender body part again.

"Oh, are you going to behave or not?!" I cried, and pushed the tail-biter away.

In response, the one using my head like a jungle gym gave my nose a playful tap.

"Oh, you guys," I said grumpily, and rolled over on my back to remove these pesky kittens. They were more nimble and flexible than I was, though, and immediately changed tack by jumping on top of my soft white belly and using it as a trampoline!

"Yay yay yay!" they shouted as they hopped up and down.

Yuck. Now I suddenly wished I hadn't eaten Sasha's kibble back at the mansion.

So I rolled over on my belly again and hunkered down, protecting myself from the onslaught. Of course now they jumped on my back, with one even dangling from my left ear.

Dooley, who'd popped over to his house next door and now came back in through the kitchen pet flap, eyed the circus with a laugh. "You guys look like you're having fun."

"I'm not having fun," I growled. "They are."

"Yay yay yay!" cried the kittens, as they jumped up and down on my back.

"How am I ever going to survive this?" I asked miserably as I tried to ignore the little tykes trampling all over me.

"Oh, they'll grow up eventually," said Dooley, who seemed to have softened to the kittens. "We did, remember?"

Frankly I couldn't remember ever having been this young and silly, but logically thinking there must have been a time when I was a kitten myself. Hard to believe, right?

"Woo-hoo!" said the one dangling from my ear, then fell down on his tush, only to immediately crawl up again and climb on top of my head for another round, this time going for my other ear.

The pet flap flapped again, and Brutus and Harriet came

strolling in. Harriet is a bright white Persian and her boyfriend Brutus a perfectly black butch cat. They've been an item for a long time and nothing can come between them—unless they come between themselves themselves, of course, if you know what I mean. But isn't that often the case?

When they saw the circus in full swing—literally—they both burst out laughing.

"Yeah, laugh all you want," I said grumpily. "It's not so funny if it happens to you."

The one dangling from my ear fell down again and this time landed on his head. Immediately I checked him for injuries, but the little dude only seemed dazed for a brief moment, and then was chasing his own tail, at last leaving mine alone for a change.

"They're very lively," said Harriet with a smile. "Who are they?"

"They were left on Odelia's doorstep this morning," said Dooley. "She's going to keep them."

Harriet's smile vanished. "Keep them? What do you mean, keep them?"

"Just what I said. She's going to keep the kittens."

"She can't do that," said Harriet, flicking a look at Brutus as if hoping he'd back her up. "Can she, sweetie pie?"

"Of course she can. It's her house—her rules. If she wants to take in an elephant or a rhinoceros who's going to stop her?"

"Animal control? I think we should have a say in this, don't you?"

Brutus shrugged. "Hey, we're just the cats. It's the humans that make the rules."

"No, but we live here, too. She can't just decide to take in three strangers and not ask our opinion. And I, for one, vote against adding to the pack." She gestured to the rest of us, the kittens meanwhile playing with one of the ping pong balls

Odelia had thrown on the floor. "Four is company, seven is a crowd. Isn't that how the saying goes?"

"More like two's company, three's a crowd," I said.

"Whatever! She can't keep adding cats. We're already overcrowded in here as it is."

"We do have two houses and two backyards," Brutus pointed out. He quickly shut up when Harriet gave him one of her death-ray glares.

"We also have the park," said Dooley, oblivious of the danger he was in. Contradicting Harriet can prove hazardous to one's physical integrity. "And the street—the entire town of Hampton Cove, really."

"Nobody asked you, Dooley," Harriet snapped.

Dooley looked confused. "But I thought you said—"

"Never mind what I said! Either *they* go, or I go. Do I make myself clear?"

"Crystal," I said, and the others murmured their agreement. Harriet had made herself so clear, in fact, that I had a feeling she was going to be sorely disappointed when Odelia told her it was her way or the highway. And why wouldn't she? This was Odelia's house, after all. Us cats might think we are in charge, but at the end of the day we simply aren't.

The kittens must have spotted Harriet, for they now came walking up to her, still a little faltering in their step.

"Don't you dare," she said in a voice that shook with indignation.

The kittens stared, clearly never having seen anything like her before.

"This fur is perfect, not a blemish. And if you so much as think about touching me… hey!"

The kittens hadn't merely thought about touching her—they'd gone and done it. More, they'd jumped on top of Harriet and were now using her for trampoline practice.

"Yay, yay, yay," they were singing as they hopped up and down.

"No! Get off! Go away! You can't—Brutus! Do something!" Harriet cried.

Brutus jumped into the fray, but to no avail. Like fleas, the kittens jumped from Harriet to Brutus and back, having a whale of a time.

"Come here, you little…" Brutus was growling, but even his foulest glare or deepest growl couldn't stop the cats from running rings around him and Harriet.

And as I watched on, I said, "Now there's a sight you don't see every day."

"No, you definitely don't," Dooley agreed.

CHAPTER 12

Odelia walked into the police station, her grandmother right on her heels, and immediately recognized in the diminutive figure of the fair-haired woman who sat on a chair in the waiting room the famous actress who'd been Jeb's first wife and loyal partner for twenty-five years, until he traded her in for a younger model in the form of Camilla. Next to Helena sat her lookalike daughter Fae. Both women got up when Odelia approached.

"So you must be Odelia," said Helena as she pressed Odelia's hand. "Fae told me what she did."

"Mom wasn't happy about it at first," Fae explained, "but she quickly warmed to the idea when she realized Dad could be in jail for the rest of his life."

"Jeb can't be in jail. He just can't. He's so sensitive. Jail will crush his soul."

"I understand," said Odelia. "The thing is, and I'm going to be totally upfront with you—I'm still not entirely convinced Jeb didn't do this."

Fae rolled her eyes. "Oh, please. Haven't you listened to a word I said? Dad isn't like that. He's not a killer."

"He was pretty doped up," Gran remarked in that subtle way of hers.

Both women turned to her. "And who are you?" asked Fae frostily.

"My name is Vesta Muffin and I'm a flogger," said Gran, extending her wrinkly, bony hand. "And I'm here to tell you that I'm gonna fight for your cause until my dying breath."

Helena eyed Gran uncertainly. "I thought you said you don't believe in our cause?"

"If you want to know what I think," said Gran, warming to her subject, "it's that your precious Jeb was high as a kite when suddenly this bimbo who'd been suing him for his last cent shows up at his door. So, being baked out of his skull on coke and meth and whatnot, he grabs a knife and stabs her to death in a frenzy the likes of which this country hasn't seen since Charlie Manson and his merry band of whacked-out psychos. Then he zonked out and when he woke up he didn't remember a thing. That's what I think happened."

"Dad would never do that," said Fae, tears springing to her eyes. "He would never kill anyone, drugs or no drugs."

"Ah, but you gotta admit he was tripping," Gran pointed out. "Now this is what you need to tell Jeb's lawyers. They can plead temporary insanity and blame it all on Jeb's drug dealer, whoever he is. He's the one they should put in jail for murder. He's the one who killed that poor woman, not Jeb, who's just another victim in this case."

"Right," said Odelia, giving her grandmother another nudge.

"Stop poking me!" Gran said. "I'm sensitive on account of the fact that I'm slim."

Odelia gave Helena and her daughter an apologetic smile. "Don't listen to my grandmother. She watches a lot of soap operas."

Uncle Alec appeared and waved them over. "Better be

quick about this, all right?" he said. "Five minutes and that's it. No extensions."

Odelia nodded and braced herself for her first encounter with the fallen superstar. The deal was that Helena and Fae had visitation rights, and Odelia would accompany them as their legal advisor, even though she didn't possess a legal bone in her body. Gran was tagging along as Odelia's plus-one, which, if anyone asked, was a tenable proposition at best.

They were led into the interview room, where Jeb Pott sat with his hands shackled to the table, head down. When they entered, he looked up. Seeing Helena and Fae, suddenly tears appeared in his eyes and trickled down his cheeks. "Helena. Fae. Darlings. I didn't do this," he said in husky tones. "You have to believe me."

"Isn't it true, Mr. Pott, that you were passed out in a drug-induced coma and don't remember a thing?" asked Gran.

"Yes, but..."

"And isn't it also true that you were found covered in your victim's blood and with the murder weapon next to you?"

"Yes, but I..."

"And isn't it also true," said Gran, raising her voice, "that you invited the poor woman to your lodge in the dead of night with the express purpose of luring her to her death?" She slammed the table. "Confess now, young man, and we can still make a deal!"

"Who the hell are you?!" Jeb cried.

"She's my grandmother," said Odelia, mortified.

Jeb directed his watery eyes on Odelia. "And who are you?"

"Odelia Poole—private detective," said Fae proudly, placing her hand on her dad's. "I hired her to clear your name, Daddy. She's going to work hard to get you out of here."

"Uh-huh," said Jeb, who seemed more confused and rattled than when he played The Prisoner of Zenda in the movie with the same name.

"I just have one question for you, Mr. Pott," said Odelia. "Did you send those texts inviting Camilla Kirby to meet you at the lodge?"

"No, of course not. Why would I want to meet that woman after what she did to me? She destroyed my life, my career—she took great pleasure turning the whole world against me and destroying everything I worked years to accomplish. And what I was most upset about," he added, softening, "is that she hurt the two people I care about most in this world: you, my darling Fae, and you, Helena. And I'm truly sorry about that."

"You do realize that accusing your ex-wife only builds a stronger case against you, don't you, sonny boy?" asked Gran, scowling and poking a crooked finger in his direction.

"Gran, please," said Odelia. "You're not working for the prosecution, you're working for the defense, remember?"

Gran frowned. "I don't get it."

Odelia decided to put it in terms her grandmother would understand. "You're Perry Mason, not Hamilton Burger."

A sly smile crept up Gran's face. "Right, right."

"More to the point, you're a vlogger helping me on a case. So you're really Paul Drake, and I am Perry Mason. Though since I'm not a lawyer but a private detective, I'm actually more like Thomas Magnum and you're either Rick or TC. Your choice."

Gran sat down. "I'm confused," she declared. "This legal mumbo-jumbo sounds a lot easier on TV than in real life."

"Tell me about it," mumbled Jeb.

"I forgive you, Jeb," said Helena. "Everything that happened between us is now in the past. What matters most is that you build yourself a stellar defense team."

"How can I?" said Jeb sadly. "I'm broke. No decent lawyer will defend a man who's got nothing but a pile of debts."

"We'll get you a lawyer, Daddy," said Fae. "Isn't that right, Mom?"

Helena hesitated. "A good defense costs a lot of money, darling. And I'm afraid it's money that we don't have."

"Then I'll pay for it. My modeling career is going well. I *want* to pay for it, Daddy," she insisted when Jeb shook his head.

"It's fine, darling. I'll manage somehow. I still have a couple of friends in the industry. I'll get the money together." He turned to Odelia. "So you're a private dick, huh?"

"She is," said Gran proudly. "My granddaughter is the best private dick this side of Long Island."

Jeb nodded gratefully. "Then I'm glad you're on my side, Miss Poole."

"You can call me Odelia," said Odelia, who was suddenly starting to feel a little giddy. Being in close proximity to the famous dreamboat actor had that effect on her. Though he didn't look as handsome as he used to in his heyday, he was still plenty charismatic.

He took her hand and fixed her with an intense look. "I promise you, Odelia. I didn't do this. Even though I may have been strung out on booze and dope, I would never kill a person, even one I hated with every fiber of my being," he said, suddenly clenching his jaw.

All in all, as Odelia walked out of the interview room, she still wasn't convinced that Jeb hadn't killed his ex-wife. On the other hand, she believed that people were innocent until proven guilty, and decided to extend Jeb that courtesy, too.

She also believed that Helena and Fae believed in Jeb. So what other choice did she have but to pursue this investigation and pursue it as if she really were the best private dick this side of Long Island?

CHAPTER 13

They were out in the parking lot, and Helena and her daughter started to walk away in the direction of their car. Odelia followed them. "If I'm going to do this I need to do it right," she said.

"Right, like the professional dicks that we are," Gran confirmed.

"What I mean is that I need to know if there's anyone out there who might hold a grudge against Jeb."

Helena laughed, and so did Fae. "Anyone? How about I write you a list?"

"That many, huh?"

"You don't become an A-list actor without making a couple of enemies along the way." She held up a hand. "Not that Jeb would ever rub anyone the wrong way or that he's difficult to work with. On the contrary. Ask anyone. He's a total sweetheart, off and on the set."

"But he does have enemies."

"There are colleagues who are jealous. Guys he started out with but who never reached the top. They could drink his blood."

"Not literally, though," Fae interjected with a laugh.

"Some could drink his blood, especially the weird ones," said her mother. "Then there's the directors he rubbed the wrong way by wanting to pursue his own creative vision when they felt otherwise."

"Yes, but those are creative differences you're talking about," said Odelia. "That and petty jealousy. But this is murder. Someone who hates Jeb so intensely that he or she would murder another human being simply to get back at Jeb."

"Or someone who hated Camilla so much and didn't care if the blame fell on Jeb," said Gran.

"Or both," Fae said. "Someone who hated my daddy and Camilla and figured out a way to get rid of them both in one fell swoop."

Odelia nodded as she thought this through. They could be looking for a person who hated Jeb or Camilla or both. At any rate, whoever this person was—if this person even existed—he or she needed to have been in the area last night. "Do you know of anyone who had a grudge against Jeb or Camilla and who is in town right now?"

Helena frowned and tapped her lips. "Well, there's our neighbor, of course. Fitz Priestley." She exchanged a look with her daughter. "He hates Jeb right now, doesn't he?"

"Oh, yes. Fitz hates Jeb *so* hard right now."

"Fitz Priestley the director? I thought Jeb was his muse?"

"He was, but that was before Jeb's name became synonymous with spousal abuse," said Helena. "Now he's box office poison and no producer or studio will come near Fitz."

"Which means," continued Fae, "that the movies Fitz made with Jeb are not being rented, not being downloaded or watched on Netflix. He's losing a lot of money. Plus, his name is now tainted by association, which is never a good thing for an ambitious director."

"But would he murder Camilla to get back at Jeb?" asked Odelia. "That seems unlikely."

"Oh, but he hated Camilla, too," said Helena. "He cast her as his leading lady in his most recent project, for a star turn along with Jeb, but with the divorce the project fell through. He'd put a lot of his own money in it, and he lost it all."

It was perhaps a reason to hate a person, but murder? Then again, stranger things had happened, Odelia thought. She made a mental note to check out this Fitz Priestley guy. Especially the fact that he lived right next door and probably knew the ins and outs of Jeb's life made this a potentially promising lead.

"Don't forget about Jeb's drug dealer," croaked Gran, earning her twin scowls from Helena and Fae. "What?" she said, raising her arms, palms up. "The man is a druggie. And we all know every drug addict needs a drug dealer. And if Jeb is as broke as he claims he is, maybe he owed his dealer a ton of money. Drug dealers don't like it when customers don't pay up. They tend to get nasty. And some of them even get murderous."

"Yes, but he would simply have roughed Jeb up if that was the case," said Helena. "Besides, I don't think Jeb has a dealer in town. He always carries his own stuff with him." When her daughter shot her a look, she blushed. "Mrs. Muffin is right, honey. Daddy does love his nose candy. And that stuff doesn't come cheap nor can you buy it at your local deli. I remember Jeb had a guy in LA, so he probably got a nice stash and brought it out here."

"And past airport security? Doubtful," said Gran.

"Daddy uses his private jet," said Fae, practically sticking out her tongue at Gran. "And private jets can smuggle as many drugs around the country as they want."

"I don't think so," said Odelia. "They have to go through

customs just like passengers on commercial airlines. Though the checks might be more cursory for a star like Jeb."

"I should never have invited Jeb here," said Helena.

"Mom!"

"But he was feeling so down after things ended with Camilla that I thought he needed a change of scene. Plus, I hoped that somehow, maybe, I could 'heal' him, you know." She laughed a curt laugh. "As if anyone has ever been able to change Jeb."

"Why change him? He's perfect the way he is," said Fae.

Helena directed a sad look at her daughter and touched her hair, with Fae brushing her hand away. Helena clearly wasn't happy that her drug-abusing ex-partner had decided to continue his self-destructive lifestyle at the lodge, setting a terrible example for Fae.

"So how long had Jeb been down here?" asked Odelia.

"Um, two months or so? He had to get out of LA, and wanted to be close to Fae. I wouldn't let him stay at the house, though, because of the drugging and the boozing."

"And the women," Fae said softly.

Her mother nodded.

"If he was here two months he must have had a local dealer," said Gran. "He wasn't slipping a bag of coke through security and he wasn't going to go without for two whole months, so we need to find his dealer, honey," she added, tapping Odelia's chest.

"You know what I think?" said Fae suddenly. "I think Camilla killed herself and then made it look like Dad did it."

"That's ridiculous, honey," said her mother. "For one thing, Camilla would never kill herself. She wasn't the type."

"She would," said Fae, nodding empathically. "To get back at Dad she would have done anything." She turned to Odelia. "Are you sure that body in the morgue is Camilla's? She could have used a lookalike, or found a dead body in the graveyard and dug it up."

"It really is Camilla," Odelia said. Though she liked Fae's out-of-the-box thinking.

Fae deflated a little, but insisted stubbornly, "You should definitely look into this. She could have cut herself, then dribbled her blood all over Dad, placed the knife next to him, then taken some sleeping pills and accidentally taken too many."

"Oh, honey," said Helena, shaking her head.

"No, but listen! Maybe she didn't mean to die, only to look so banged up Daddy would have gone to prison for a long time. Only she miscalculated and died—which was just what she deserved."

"Fae," said Helena sharply. "I never liked Camilla, but she didn't deserve to die."

Fae shrugged and crossed her arms. "Just a theory. You are going to check it out, though, aren't you, Odelia?"

Odelia assured her she would. Though if there had been sleeping pills in Camilla's stomach the coroner would have definitely found them.

"Chief Alec told me cause of death was stab wounds, sweetie," said Helena. "Not sleeping pills. And a woman as self-absorbed as Camilla would never stab herself, not even to frame an ex-husband she hated."

"I guess not," said Fae, moping a little. It's never fun to have your brilliant ideas shot down, especially when you're trying to save your beloved father from life in prison.

"Trust me," said Gran now, patting the young woman on the arm. "We're going to catch this killer and we're going to make sure he fries in the chair."

"There is no death penalty in the state of New York," said Fae with a little grin. "But I like your attitude, old lady. So points for effort."

"Old lady my foot," grumbled Gran as they walked away. "How old does she think I am? A hundred?"

"She's young, Gran," said Odelia. "Young people think that anyone over forty is ancient. Heck, I am probably an old lady to her, and so is her mom."

"Impertinence," Gran said. "If she were my daughter I'd have knocked some sense into her a long time ago."

"She's a teenager who's scared her daddy will go to jail for the rest of his life."

"She's a spoiled brat is what she is." Then she relented. "She does love her daddy though, which kinda got to me when I saw the two of them together in there."

It had gotten to Odelia, too. "Are you sure we can pull this off?"

"Sure I'm sure. All we need to do is follow the clues and we'll find the bastard that did this."

"Unless you're right and Jeb really did kill his ex-wife in a drug-induced frenzy."

Gran shrugged her bony shoulders. "I may have changed my mind on that."

"Oh, you have, have you? And why is that?"

"Like I said, the kid got to me. Besides, you have to trust your gut. And my gut is telling me he didn't do it. It's also telling me I'm starving, so are you going to drive me home now or what?"

"Okay, fine, we're going," she said, aiming her key fob at her pickup and listening for the telltale beep beep. "Talk about a spoiled brat," she muttered under her breath.

"I heard that!"

"Good. I wanted you to," she said as she got in.

"You better show some respect for your elders, young lady, or else."

"Or else what? You're going to denounce me on your vlog?"

"Oh, darn it!"

"What?"

Gran held up her phone. "Forgot to film the interview!"

And a good thing, too, Odelia thought as she put the car in gear. She needed her grandmother vlogging her way through this investigation like she needed a hole in the head.

"Maybe you should give up this vlog," she suggested, waving to Helena and Fae as they pulled out in front of her and merged into traffic.

"I'll never give up flogging," Gran said stubbornly. "I live to flog."

And wasn't that the truth.

CHAPTER 14

That night, Odelia was chopping tomatoes while watching something on her iPad, the frown cutting her brows indicating absolute focus. When she's working on a case she's often like that: utter concentration. I admire that about her. I sometimes have to contend with a lack of focus. Then again, I am continually faced with a lot of distractions, and I was looking at three of those distractions at that exact moment, namely Bim, Bam and Bom.

Odelia had finally named the kittens, which I thought was a dangerous sign. It meant she was probably going to keep them. I wasn't particularly fond of the names either. Who wants to be called Bom for the rest of his life, unless they plan to be a suicide bomber?

Bam was dangling from the curtains, Bim was trying to remove all the water from my bowl with her paws, and Bom, living up to his name, was climbing the couch and dive-bombing into the deep, landing on the plush carpet every time he did. He was having a ball.

They still weren't talking, which I guess was a good thing. I'd never realized kittens only babble in nonsensical vowels and consonants until they're a little older. Then again, human babies don't conduct entire conversations when they're in the cradle either, right? And they're supposed to be the top species on the planet.

"Listen to this, you guys," said Odelia now, reading from her iPad. "Jeb's last movie completely bombed at the box office, even though it had cost a quarter of a billion dollars to make, causing the studio that had green-lit the movie to file for bankruptcy, and the woman whose series of books the movie was based on to lose a big chunk of her fortune. Like Fitz Priestley, she put her own money into the production, and lost it all. She's allegedly furious with Jeb for allowing himself to be dragged into this whole divorce thing and blames him for ending her Hollywood ambitions and putting a huge dent into her bank account."

"Ouch," I commented.

Odelia looked up triumphantly. "And guess what? She has a second home in Hampton Cove! So she could easily be behind this whole thing."

"Who is this writer?" I asked.

"Prunella Lemon. She wrote those *Chronicles of Zeus* novels. About a young girl, Ellie Zeus, who accidentally discovers her father is actually the Greek god Zeus and she has all these godlike powers. Jeb played her mentor, the quirky genius inventor Florida Stopper."

"Right," I said. I'd heard about those. They were a big success back when they were published, almost as popular as *Harry Potter*. I hoped they hadn't put a nasty cat in them, though, like Mrs. Norris in the Potter books. Creatures like that give us cats a bad name.

Brutus and Harriet came trudging through the cat flap. But when Harriet saw the cavorting kittens, she hesitated, then cut a curious glance to Odelia. "Um, Odelia?" she said.

"Mh?" said Odelia, still reading on her tablet, while her tomatoes had been reduced to pulp by her unfocused hand.

"About those kittens?"

"Uh-huh?"

"Are we, um, going to have them with us for a long time? I mean, can you give us a time frame? Just so we know how long we'll be able to enjoy their pleasant company?"

Odelia was still frowning. "Listen to this. 'Jeb Pott was the wrong choice to cast as Florida Stopper. If I'd known then what I know now, I'd never have asked him. He's the reason this project turned into an absolute nightmare.'" She looked up. "Prunella Lemon."

"Yes, that's all very interesting," said Harriet, "but what about the kittens? We do love those little babies so much, and we're hoping they can be with us for... a day? A week?"

"I can't believe this," said Odelia, shaking her head. "I mean, Jeb has so many enemies you wouldn't believe. And anyone could have sent those text messages to Camilla, right? Or greeted her at the door while Jeb was passed out in bed."

"Whoever this person is would have had to have intimate knowledge of Jeb's habits," I said. "His whereabouts, the fact that he was drugged out most of the time. And Camilla's private number so they could text her, pretending to be Jeb, and lure her into a trap."

"You're right absolutely right, Max," said Odelia, nodding. "Which still makes me wonder if Jeb isn't the one behind this after all. I mean, the simplest solution is often the right one, right? Camilla ruined him. She destroyed his life and his career. So maybe he thought he'd lost everything anyway so why not kill her and get it over with?"

"He loves his daughter, though," said Dooley. "So maybe for her sake he wouldn't have gone through with something like that."

"Also a good point," said Odelia, who was on fire now. And so was whatever she was cooking in the oven. Black smoke was wafting from the door and escaping into the room.

"Fire!" cried Brutus. "The oven is on fire!"

"Oh, no!" said Odelia, grabbing a towel. She yanked open the oven door, took out her dish and plunked it down on the ceramic cooktop then stared at it. It did not look edible.

At that exact moment, Chase walked in. "Hey, babe. Oh, hell," he said, and hurried over to assist Odelia in handling this minor kitchen disaster.

"Hey!" suddenly shouted Harriet, and we all looked up, even Chase. "Will you listen to me?! How long?! Are these cats?! Going to stay here?! A week?! A month?! Or forever?!"

CHAPTER 15

That night, cat choir was a sad affair. Harriet, after flipping her lid, hadn't wanted to come, and neither had Brutus, since he needed to stay home to appease his girlfriend. So it was just me and Dooley, and frankly we weren't in the mood for a whole lot of singing and gossiping either. Not while there were three little ones at home wrecking the house and eating all of our food. Plus, we needed to figure out who would want to hurt Jeb Pott, and I didn't think I was going to glean a lot of new information about Jeb or his ex-wife by shooting the breeze with Hampton Cove's cat population.

Of course I was wrong.

The first clue I got that maybe we were onto something was when Clarice showed up for cat choir. Clarice is a feral cat who roams the streets of Hampton Cove for food and often stays out in the forest that edges our small town. She may be feral but she's also our friend, which sometimes surprises me, as she's one of those cats who eat rats whole without even bothering to chew. She simply gobbles them down, if you know what I mean. One moment they are there, and when you blink they're gone. Down the hatch. It's the weirdest thing.

"Boys," she growled when she caught sight of us. "Have I got news for you."

Clarice never had news for us. Not unless she got something in return. Like food.

"Hey, Clarice," Dooley said. "We have kittens at home now. Three of them."

Clarice shot Dooley a look that could kill, then continued, "Word on the street is that your grandmother has been popping pills like there's no tomorrow."

I laughed. "That's ridiculous. Gran would never pop pills."

Clarice wasn't laughing, though. She didn't even crack a smile. "Listen, you idiot. I'm only telling you this because your family has been good to me. Your human gave me a home, and even though I don't care about a home, or the trappings of domestication, I still think the gesture was pretty cool. So shut up and listen."

I shut up and listened, and so did Dooley.

"There's this guy. He's selling all kinds of nasty stuff to your granny. And if she takes that stuff she's going to fire up like a rocket and then she's going to crash and burn, if you know what I mean." She cocked a meaningful whisker at me and I nodded quickly.

"Oh, sure," I said. "Go up and go down and crash and then burn. I get it. Totally."

"Who's going up, Max?" asked Dooley.

"Gran is going up because of something she bought off some guy."

"Listen, you idiots," Clarice snarled. "Your Granny has to be stopped. That stuff isn't candy. And if she keeps taking it she's going to die, understand?"

I laughed a light laugh. "Oh, Clarice. You don't know Gran like we do. That woman is indestructible."

"Yes," laughed Dooley, as lightly as I did. "She can't be destroyed, even if you tried."

"Listen!" Clarice growled. "You morons aren't getting what I'm saying. Granny is in danger. And now I've said too much already."

"Too much?" I had the feeling she hadn't said a thing. "That's all right," I said. "We won't tell a soul." Mainly because I had no idea what she'd just said.

"Except Granny, of course," said Dooley. "We'll tell her about the rocket, won't we, Max?"

"Oh, yes. We'll tell her all about the rocket. And the up and the down and—"

"Don't tell your granny!" Clarice hissed. "Tell Odelia. She'll know what I'm talking about. Ecstasy!" she added emphatically, pointing towards the sky, then the ground.

We followed her movements keenly, staring first up and then down. I still had no idea what she was trying to say, but I was smiling and nodding as if I got the message.

"Copy that, Clarice," I said, tapping my nose and giving her a meaningful wink.

"Oh, why do I even bother?" Clarice grumbled, then stalked off again, leaving behind two very bewildered cats.

"Did you understand a word she was saying?" asked Dooley.

"Nope. Something about going up and going down and crashing and burning."

"I hate it when she speaks in riddles, don't you?"

"Hate it," I agreed.

And then we joined the others: Shanille, our director, Kingman, Milo, the cat that belongs to the neighbor across the street, Big Mac, a cat who likes... Big Macs, and of course Tom and Tigger and Misty and Shadow and Buster and Darlene and all the others. We're a tight-knit community, us Hampton Cove cats, and soon choir practice began and we all sang our little hearts out, Shanille on top of the jungle gym, and the rest of us spread out across the playground the Hampton Cove council was so kind to install in the park.

I think it was probably aimed at entertaining kids and providing them with a measure of exercise. But we make good use of it, too. Nearby the ducks were quacking softly, Rita the owl was hooting, and for a brief moment I forgot all about Bim, Bam and Bom, and Jeb Pott and Harriet blowing her top. I mean, who needs a shrink when you can sing at the top of your lungs along with a bunch of other nocturnal animals, right?

But then a well-aimed size-14 shoe hit me straight on the noggin and I dropped from my high perch and fell to the rubber mulch below.

Could this be what Clarice had meant about Gran going up and then going down?

Had Gran joined a choir that was as unpopular with her neighbors as ours?

CHAPTER 16

"I don't know about this, babe," Chase was saying.

Odelia and her burly cop were seated on the salon couch, watching *The Voice*. The coaches were bickering, the candidates were singing out of tune, and generally the whole thing failed to grip. Odelia knew it had more to do with the case she'd accepted than the quality of the show, but she still turned down the sound. "About Jeb Pott, you mean?"

He nodded, absentmindedly caressing the three kittens that had fallen asleep on his lap.

Odelia smiled. "For a dog person you're awfully good with cats."

"I'm a pet person. Dogs, cats, goldfish. I adapt. Where are Max and Dooley, by the way?" he asked, looking around.

"Cat choir," she said before she could stop herself. "I mean, the park. I think. They like to roam around there at night, meeting other cats, doing what cats do. At least, I think they do. It's not as if they confide in me, you know," she added with a nervous little laugh.

He gave her a curious look. "Look, this is an open-and-shut case, Odelia. Jeb did it. He killed his ex-wife and that's it.

But you offering your services to his daughter, that just seems... wrong."

"I didn't offer my services. In fact I didn't know I had any services to offer. She came to me, remember?"

"Still. She's offering you money to prove her dad is innocent, while you know as well as I do that he's guilty. You're giving her false hope, babe. And at some point you're going to have to disappoint her, and you're going to feel bad about accepting her money."

"I'm not going to accept any money. I'm just doing this to satisfy my personal curiosity. There are certain things that are not jibing with the official version of events."

"The burner phones," he said, nodding. "But is it so hard to believe that a movie star like Jeb would possess a disposable phone? Heck, I'll bet he's got dozens he uses for various purposes. These are the same people who change phone numbers the way they change underwear, just in case some media person gets a hold of it and starts pestering them. Or some stalker fan. They're notoriously paranoid and often for good reason."

She had to admit he had a point. But how could she explain she had a gut feeling that there was something not completely right about this case? That it was perhaps too open-and-shut? She couldn't, so she decided not to even try. "I guess I'll just prove you right in the end," she said instead. "In which case, no harm done. And in the event that there is something more to the case than meets the eye, I'd like to think I'll find it."

"Good luck," he said wryly. "And is it true that your grandmother is assisting you?"

"That is true, and she's doing a pretty good job so far." Chase didn't seem convinced. She gave him a playful poke in the ribs. "There's something else bothering you, isn't there? I know you well enough by now to know that when you get all broody like this you've got something on your mind. And I'm pretty sure it's not me poking around your case."

"It's not," he conceded. He shifted a little, careful not to wake up the kittens.

It was such an adorable sight: the burly cop with the tiny kittens buried in his big arms. Her heart melted from the sheer tenderness the homey scene displayed.

"The thing is..." He swallowed.

Uh-oh. He really did have something on his mind. "Just cut to the chase... Chase," she quipped.

"All right. The thing is that... I talked to your cats the other day. And I got the impression they talked right back to me."

Double uh-oh. She gulped a little. "What do you mean?"

He shrugged, displacing the kittens. They changed position but went on sleeping, nestling closer against his chest. "I said something and they meowed something. Then I said something else and they meowed some more. And each time I said something or asked a question, they answered. It was the darndest thing."

"What did you ask them?"

"I asked 'Max, can you understand me?' And he responded!"

She smiled. "That happens to me all the time. Some cats are very talkative. You say something and they immediately respond. That doesn't mean they can actually understand what you're saying. Or that we can understand what they're saying."

"No, but the other day when you were in the hospital? Your mom or grandma said something and I had the impression they actually understood when your cats responded."

"Oh, that's just Mom and Gran. They love those cats so much they pretend to talk to them all the time." She felt a trickle of sweat drip down her spine. How was she going to salvage this? "It's the women in this family. We're crazy about cats. You know that, right?"

"Yeah, of course I know that. It's a part of you I adore. I mean, the little fellas never meant much to me before. But ever since I met you, and your cats, there's just something… special about the bond you share. Something I can't seem to put my finger on."

"But you're okay with it, right?"

"Oh, sure. I think it's pretty damn cute." He smiled and leaned in for a quick peck on her lips. "I almost can't believe it myself, but I'm actually starting to like the little fellas myself. Not as much as you, obviously, or your mom and gran, but I have to admit I'd miss them if they were gone. How crazy is that, right?"

"Not crazy at all," she said. "Cats are intelligent creatures. Sometimes I think they understand us a lot better than perhaps we understand ourselves. The way they're always listening, watching, observing us. I think they're very wise animals, and maybe that's why we're so fond of them."

"Well, I'm definitely turning into a crazy cat dude," he said with a chuckle.

One of the kittens had woken up and gazed up at Chase, then whispered, "Dada?"

Odelia stifled a cry of surprise. "Oh, Chase," she said, placing her hand on his arm.

"I know, babe," he said softly, then pressed a kiss to the top of her head, and tickled the kitten under the chin until it fell asleep again.

CHAPTER 17

Gran was up early. Which wasn't unusual for her. In fact she often got up before the crack of dawn. When the rest of the world was still fast asleep she was already pottering about in her nightgown. Maybe it was because of her age, but she preferred it that way. She felt most productive in the early morning hours and felt she could get a lot more done.

Like working in her backyard—though technically it was Tex and Marge's backyard—and checking her tomato plants or the lettuce she'd planted a while back. She'd always loved the idea of a kitchen garden so she'd created one. It was just a tiny patch of green but it was hers, and so far it had yielded radishes, peas, spring onions, garlic and the highly-anticipated tomatoes and lettuce. She had big plans for her garden, and hoped to expand it so she could sell some of her produce on the farmer's market. Anything to supplement her meager pension and the paltry allowance she got from her penny-pinching son-in-law.

Today she wasn't to be found in the backyard, though, in spite of the fact that the sun was already hoisting itself over the horizon and the day promised to be a scorcher. She wasn't even moving about in the kitchen, preparing a cake or breakfast. No, today Vesta Muffin could be found hovering over her laptop and cursing at the screen. For her big rival Scarlett Canyon had posted yet another Instagram story where she displayed her knack for making herself the center of attention. She'd filmed herself on the beach, showcasing a new line of beachwear she was modeling for Darling's Dress Code, one of the local boutiques that were so popular with the celebrity crowd that flocked to the Hamptons every summer.

Gwyneth Paltrow, Christie Brinkley and her daughters, Nina Agdal, Malia Obama, Hailey Baldwin, Rachel Zoe… They all loved to shop at Darling's Dress Code and showcase the shop's unique designs on their social media.

And now Scarlett had joined that illustrious line of celebrity influencers and was garnering hundreds of comments and thousands of likes in the process.

Gran ground her teeth as she watched the video. Even though Scarlett was her age, she still looked like a supermodel, with her impossible waistline and her Kardashian-type bust. All surgically enhanced, of course, but tell that to the idiots who flocked to her Instagram with dullard comments about how 'hawt' Scarlett looked.

"Hawt my ass," Gran grumbled under her breath. "More like a painted tart."

She checked her own YouTube page. A whopping seventy-five followers, three down from the day before.

As she sat back, she thought about the kind of stunt she would have to pull to crank up her popularity in the flogging space. So far she'd only flogged sporadically. Once every couple of weeks she would upload a video, mostly showcasing herself explaining what she'd been up to as the executive assistant to her granddaughter, Hampton Cove's very own super sleuth, or her son, Hampton Cove's chief of police. Or even playing scrabble behind the reception desk at Tex's office or helping her daughter set up the library for one of her book club events. It was becoming clear to her that this kind of stuff didn't cut it. If she was going to make a splash in the flogging community she would have to switch things up. Flog some more and maybe stop filming herself and film some of the stuff people really wanted to see. And what did people want to see? Blood and gore. And lots and lots of drama. Tragedy.

People naturally were rubberneckers. When there was a car crash, long lines would form and people would take out their phones to film the whole thing. Why else did shows like *Game of Thrones* attract such a massive following? Blood and gore and the prospect of people suffering horrific deaths at every turn.

"People are sadists," she said as she absentmindedly caressed Harriet.

The white Persian had been spending all of her time at the house, which didn't surprise Gran. Usually she was over at Odelia's a lot, but ever since her granddaughter had taken in three kittens, Harriet had taken refuge at Tex and Marge and Vesta's.

"Tell me about it," said Harriet. "Doesn't Odelia realize how much damage those kittens are causing? Not to mention the emotional distress."

"Mh," said Gran, not really paying the grumpy cat a lot of attention. "I think I need to showcase some of the more gory aspects of this detective business," she said. "Maybe then people will finally tune in and give me the attention I deserve."

"And then there's Max and Dooley, who have totally given up the fight. Almost as if they like kittens. Nobody likes kittens, unless they're human."

"Maybe I could go over to the coroner's office and get a couple of shots of the dead girl," said Gran, a grim set to her face. "And if I could only convince that bonehead son of mine to send me some grisly pictures of the crime scene my flogging career would finally take off like a rocket." With these words, she popped another little white pill into her mouth.

Almost immediately she felt the boost. These vitamins she'd purchased off a street vendor were a real lifesaver. Ever since she'd started taking them, she had so much energy she felt like she could take over the world.

"Can't you talk Odelia into giving up those three menaces, Gran?"

"Mh?" asked Gran. "What's that, toots?"

"The kittens," said Harriet with an expressive eyeroll. "We need to get rid of the kittens."

Gran frowned. She wasn't following. "Get rid of the kittens? Why would you want to get rid of the kittens? They're the cutest thing since you and Max and Dooley were kittens yourselves."

"Oh, Gran," said Harriet. "I was never a kitten. I came into this world fully formed."

"Honey, you were most definitely a kitten once. And if I'm totally honest, you were even cuter than those three, but also a lot more annoying."

Harriet stared at her, aghast. "Impossible. I was never annoying."

"All kittens are annoying, especially when they dig up your geraniums and pee all over your tomato plants. But they're so cute you forgive them for everything."

Harriet placed her head on her front paws. "Still. We need to get rid of these three."

Gran shook her head. "Harriet, honey. Sometimes you scare me."

But then she forgot all about her cat's petty gripes and focused on the task at hand: shooting the kind of footage people were dying to watch. And how she was going to accomplish that particular feat. As she thought, she popped another pill into her mouth.

She giggled when she felt the kick.

Boy, oh, boy. If only she'd discovered these vitamins sooner, she could have been president of the country. Better yet, she could have ruled the world. Or even the universe!

CHAPTER 18

The next morning, bright and early, Odelia was up even before me and Dooley. Even Chase was up, and he was usually the slower riser.

"Weird," said Dooley, lifting his weary head. "When the humans start waking up before we do, you know there's something wrong, Max."

"I hear you, Dooley," I said, yawning. And that's when I saw them: the three kittens were lying between me and Dooley. Bim had her teeth clamped down on my tail and was gently chewing it, Bam was lying on his back, his paws dangling in the air, and Bom was resting his head on Dooley's hindquarters.

We both stared at the threesome for a moment, then Dooley said softly, "They're actually pretty cute when they're asleep."

"The key word being 'asleep,'" I grunted.

"Oh, don't be such a curmudgeon, Max," said Odelia, who was rooting around in her sock drawer.

"I'm not. They're annoying is what they are."

"They're not. Just look at them! They're so cute!"

And she was off again, with the gibberish. Ugh.

"For one thing, they can't stop biting my tail," I said.

"They think it's a pacifier," said Odelia.

I didn't even know what a pacifier was, nor was I interested to find out.

"Second, they climb the curtains, they pee in the plants, they dig for the roots, they eat my food, they drop little balls of paper into my water bowl… Do I have to go on?"

"All true, but they're also very, very cute," she said, and tickled Bom until he giggled and crowed with delight.

Ugh. Yes, they were. Even I, official member of the Cat Curmudgeon Club, had to admit that kittens were cute.

"Harriet wants to know how long they're going to stay," said Dooley. "I don't think she likes them a lot either."

"Harriet is a curmudgeon, too, and so is Brutus and so are you, Dooley. There's actually a lot you can learn from these little guys. They're playful, they don't grumble or nag, they're still looking at the world with wondrous eyes and they're so, so cuuuuuute!"

"You're doing it again, babe," said Chase, walking in from the bathroom. He had casually slapped a towel around his waist, and was displaying that finely honed musculature some human females go all gaga over—almost as gaga as they go over babies or, yes, kittens.

Odelia went gaga now, jumping into Chase's arms. "I'm a crazy cat lady, you told me so yourself, crazy cat dude!"

"Yes, but they're so cuuuuute!" he said with a wide grin.

Kissing ensued, and Dooley and I dutifully covered the kittens' eyes.

They did not need to see this.

"So Clarice told us something weird last night," I said when Chase had disappeared down the stairs to start breakfast.

"Oh? What did she say?"

"She said Gran is taking pills and going up and then going down."

"She's also crashing and burning," said Dooley. "Like a rocket."

Odelia frowned. "Pills? What pills?"

"They're not what she thinks they are," said Dooley.

"She mentioned ecstasy?" I said.

"Oh, my God," Odelia muttered. "Are you sure that's the word she used?"

"Uh-huh. Pretty sure. Ecstasy. Overwhelming feeling of great joy?" Gran had never struck me as a particularly ecstatic person, but then maybe she had her moments in private.

"Ecstasy is a drug. People take it so they can party long and hard. It gives you an energy boost and a sense of euphoria but it's highly addictive and can also make you very, very sick. If Gran is taking ecstasy, she shouldn't. How did Clarice know?"

I shrugged. "She didn't say. But you know Clarice. She has her sources."

"Just like me," said Odelia with a smile. "Thanks for the warning, you guys. Looks like Gran is buying something off some guy that she shouldn't. I wonder why she didn't tell me."

"Have you made any progress with the case?" I asked.

"Not much. Today I'm going to start interviewing people. Wanna come?"

"Oh, sure," I said, my heart making a little jump of joy. Anything to be away from these three cuuuuuuute kittens.

Yes, I know. I'm a curmudgeon. But a cuteness overdose is just as bad as an overdose from that stuff that Gran takes, don't you think? No? Well, that proves you're not ready to become a member of the Cat Curmudgeon Club.

Odelia scooped up the kittens and headed downstairs, followed by yours truly and Dooley. In the kitchen, Chase was pouring himself and Odelia cups of coffee.

"Mh," Odelia said as she looked down at the three balls of fur. "I don't want to leave them alone and I don't think I should take them along with me. What to do?"

"Don't look at me," Chase said. "I may be crazy cat dude now, but I'm not ready to tell your uncle I can't come to work because I have to babysit a bunch of cats."

"Can't you take them to work?" she asked.

He narrowed his eyes at her. "Is this a test?"

"No test," she said with a grin as she placed the kittens on the counter and her arms around Chase's neck. "I just don't feel comfortable leaving them alone all day. And since I'm not going to be in the office much today…"

"Conducting your big investigation, huh?"

"Exactly."

He lifted his shoulders in a shrug. "Okay, sure. I'll take them. And in case I have to go out, I'll just leave them at the desk with Dolores. That sound like a plan to you?"

"Perfect," she said.

"At least they're not joining us for the investigation," Dooley whispered.

"I heard that," Odelia whispered back when Chase's back was turned.

"I heard that," said Chase.

"Chase knows I talk to you guys from time to time," said Odelia, taking a bite from the piece of toast he offered her. "And he's fine with that, isn't he?"

"Of course I'm fine with it," said Chase. "And I'm also fine with the notion that cats are intelligent creatures that respond when you talk to them. Isn't that right, Max?"

"Absolutely, Chase," I said.

Chase grinned widely. "See? What did I tell you? Max is a talker!"

"Oh, yes, he is. A big talker," said Odelia.

"Too bad we'll never know what they're saying, huh?"

"Yeah, too bad," said Odelia, and gave me a fat wink.

CHAPTER 19

I woke up from my cat nap when someone danced on my stomach. From time to time I like to rest on my back, my head slumped to the side. You might think this is an uncomfortable position but it's not. At least not for me. Today, though, it was particularly uncomfortable because, as I said, someone was using my belly for ballroom dancing practice. And even before I opened my eyes I knew exactly who that someone was.

"Bom," I grunted. "Can you please not do that? Ooph," I added when he landed on my stomach and then tumbled off and fell to the floor next to the couch.

Worried, I glanced over, only to find the little furball scrambling around on the carpet, a little dazed but otherwise still in one piece.

"There must be a guardian angel for kittens," I muttered.

"Oh, yes, there is," said Dooley as he, too, was contending with a kitten using him as an inflatable bouncy castle. In his case it was Bam. The little kitten was giggling as he playfully slapped at Dooley's face, the gray cat languidly allowing this abuse to continue.

"You know? I'm actually starting to like the little ones," I said.

"Me, too," Dooley admitted as he gave Bam a good-natured slap back and the kitten immediately engaged into a slapfest with the much bigger cat.

"I never thought I'd say this," I continued, "but they're pretty darn cute, aren't they?"

Only now did I notice that instead of three kittens, there were only two present and accounted for. I could see Bom, making valiant attempts to climb back on the couch and failing, and Bam, sitting on top of Dooley's head, with Dooley giggling as loudly as the kitten.

"Where is Bim?" I asked, suddenly worried.

"Oh, she's probably around," said Dooley, rolling over and pinning the tiny cat underneath his paw, before allowing him to escape again and climb his back.

"Yeah, but I don't see her anywhere," I said, getting up and glancing around.

Odelia and Chase were getting ready for work and paid us no mind, and of Harriet and Brutus there was no trace.

I jumped from the couch—or rather allowed my weight to drop me down, and went in search of the absent Bim. That was the trouble with kittens: you had to watch them like a hawk or else they snuck off and got themselves into all kinds of trouble.

I quickly trod up the stairs and searched the bedroom, then the guest bedroom, which had once been Gran's, but found no trace of the red-and-white kitten. The bathroom was devoid of life, too, and so was the landing.

Huh. Where could little Bim be?

I plonked down the stairs again, and bleated, "Biiiiiiim! Where are you?!"

I looked around the living room, the salon, the kitchen,

and the small storage room off the kitchen, where Odelia keeps the washer and dryer and whatever junk she can't fit into the rest of the house. And then my eye fell on the pet flap.

Oh, no. Had Bim gone outside when no one was looking?

Had she ventured out into that big scary world and gotten into trouble?

The thought scared me half to death. I immediately wormed myself through the cat flap—it had been custom-made for me but it must have shrunk since then because I was finding it harder and harder to slip through.

"Bim!" I yelled once I was out in the backyard. "Where are youuuuuu?!"

Could she have gone out into the street? I didn't dare think such a horrible thought. The street was full of cars, and those drivers rarely bothered to stop when a little ball of fluff suddenly rolled in front of their tires. For all I knew Bim had been flattened by one of those giant steel monsters.

"Biiiiiim!" I repeated.

My eye fell on the garden shed. The door to the modest wooden structure was ajar. I ventured thither and squeezed myself through the door to take a look inside. It was pretty dark in there, tools neatly dangling from pegboards on the wall, the lawnmower resting in a corner, and a workbench set up where Chase liked to mess around with stuff. Right now he was fixing up his bike, which was hanging from two hooks attached to the ceiling.

There was no sign of Bim there either, though.

Suddenly, a sound came from outside.

"Max? Is that you?" asked the voice.

I quickly emerged from the darkness of the shed. Brutus was lying underneath the hedge that divides Odelia's backyard from Tex and Marge's.

"Brutus? What are you doing there?" I asked.

Brutus looked distinctly ill at ease. He then opened his paws. And there, safe in the crook of his front legs, was Bim, sleeping peacefully, a smile on her funny little face.

"Don't tell Harriet," said Brutus hoarsely. "But I've been here since she fell asleep last night."

I smiled at the sight of the unlikely twosome. The butch cat, and the tiny fuzzball.

"I take it they've gotten to you, too, huh?"

"They're so cute," said Brutus warmly.

"They are, aren't they?"

"The thing is, Max, I know I'm, you know, fixed..."

"Yeah, me too."

We both gulped uncomfortably at the thought.

"So I've never given much thought to, you know, offspring and all that stuff."

"Me neither."

"But being around these kittens," he continued, "has kinda made me want to be a better cat."

"Same thing here, buddy," I admitted.

It was hard to believe, but Bim, Bam and Bom had somehow activated our paternal instincts. I'd never even known I had those before, and clearly neither had Brutus.

"Now all we need to do," I said, "is convince Harriet these little sweeties are not the scourge she thinks they are."

"Good luck with that," Brutus said. "If she knew I was here she'd kill me."

"Maybe not kill you, exactly, but she probably wouldn't be happy about it."

"So let's keep this our little secret, shall we, Max?"

"Sure thing," I said.

And then we watched as Bim opened her little eyes, yawned and stretched her little limbs, and stared up at the both of us. And then she licked Brutus's face. And we melted.

And I finally understood why humans love kittens so much.

It's almost impossible not to.

CHAPTER 20

Odelia, as she tootled along the road, went over her checklist in her head.

Chase had bundled up Bim, Bam and Bom and dropped them off at the vestibule to be watched over by Dolores. Check.

Max and Dooley were in the back of the car with her. Check.

She'd arranged to meet Prunella Lemon at the Riviera Country Club where apparently the bestselling authoress liked to spend her leisure time. Check.

Only one more item on her list had yet to be addressed. And she planned to do that right now. She glanced over to her grandmother, who was riding shotgun.

"You seem a little on edge, Gran," she said with a frown.

Gran had her face practically plastered to the windscreen, a strange flush suffusing her cheeks. Droplets of sweat stood out on her brow, and she had a hunted look in her eyes, which were stretched wide open.

"I'm just excited to get cracking on this murder case thingy again," croaked Gran.

Odelia cleared her throat. This was not an easy subject to broach. "The thing is, someone told me something this morning that's got me a little worried."

"Oh?"

"It's actually to do with you."

"Huh." Gran didn't look up. She was still staring unblinkingly at the road ahead.

"Is it true that you've been buying pills from some guy on the street?"

"Sure!" said Gran, much to Odelia's surprise. She'd expected her grandmother to deny the charge hotly.

"But, Gran, how could you? Don't you know how bad those pills are? Think about your heart!"

"It's my heart I was thinking about when I bought them."

"What do you mean? Those pills can kill you. They jack up your heart rate."

For the first time, Gran looked up. And Odelia saw her pupils were dilated.

"Kill me? Are you nuts? Those pills are a treat. Without those pills I'd only have half the energy I have now. They're great. And besides, if you don't like em take it up with Tex."

"My dad? What do you mean?"

"He's the one who told me to take them!"

"Dad prescribed them?"

"Of course! I was telling him only the other day how tired I felt sometimes, and he said that was only natural at my age. When I told him where to stick his disgusting ageism, he quickly climbed down from his high horse and prescribed me those pills. But when I went to fill the prescription, and the pharmacist told me how much they were going to set me back, I told him to go to hell with his crazy prices. And that's when I heard about Conrad."

"Conrad? Who's Conrad?"

"Oh, he's a miracle worker. I first heard about him from

Dick Bernstein and Rock Horowitz. The boys from the senior center? Dick has been buying from Conrad for years. Viagra. So when I complained to Dick how expensive my pills were, he told me to go and see Conrad. He gave me his number and I met him the next day at Café Baron, that new hipster bar on Downey Street? And there he was, holding forth and hawking his wares. And he couldn't have been nicer or more understanding. Gave me a big discount on my first buy."

"Oh, Gran..."

"What? I've never felt better! In fact I've got so much energy I could run for president. I mean, if all those old dudes can run for president so can I, right? I'm younger than half of them! And it's time we got a senior citizen in the White House to represent all the senior citizens in this country. I can do a lot of good from the Oval Office, you know."

"Of course you can," said Odelia, hoping her grandmother wasn't serious about this latest bee in her bonnet. "Can I take a look at those pills?"

"Sure. Here, take one. You're not looking too hot yourself this morning."

Odelia ignored the dig. She'd been up early, what with the kittens wriggling and squirming at the foot of her bed. She checked the pillbox. It had a big red X on the side.

"Gran," she said sternly, "are you sure Dad prescribed you ecstasy? Don't lie to me."

Gran looked confused. "Ecstasy? Is that the brand? They're just vitamins, honey."

"These are not vitamins. This is ecstasy. A drug. And a very nasty one, too."

Grandma laughed. "Vitamins are not drugs. Vitamins are good for you."

"How many have you taken?"

"Oh, I take them all the time," said Gran, her leg shaking

violently now, as she tapped her fingers nervously. "Popped one this morning. You can't overdose on vitamins." And with these words, she grabbed the bottle from Odelia's hand, popped the top and dropped a pill into her mouth.

"Spit it out!" Odelia cried, pulling over onto the shoulder.

"What? Are you crazy?"

"Spit it out now!"

"I don't wanna!"

"Right now!" she said, holding out her hand.

Reluctantly, Gran spat out the pill. "You're not going to deprive an old lady of her vitamins, are you? I need my vitamins."

"They're not vitamins, Gran. These are highly addictive, very dangerous pills. You could easily have overdosed on them."

"What are you talking about? Tex prescribed them for me."

"He prescribed vitamins, and then Conrad sold you ecstasy!"

"But Conrad said—"

"He's a drug dealer! He probably sells all kinds of drugs."

Gran looked annoyed, clutching her purse now. "Damn cheating bastard. I'm gonna ask for my money back. He can't do this to a little old lady."

Gran was only a little old lady when it suited her, but Odelia decided not to get sucked into an argument. It was bad enough her grandmother was a pill-popping ecstasy addict. "I'm going to take you to see my dad."

"I just saw him last week!"

"You're going to see him again. In fact you're going to see him right now," she said, making a swift decision, then performing a U-turn and heading back into town. Prunella Lemon would just have to wait.

"But I don't wanna see Tex!"

"You should have thought of that before you started taking drugs!"

"I thought they were vitamins!"

"Well, they're not, and now you're going to see the doctor. Who knows what that stuff has done to your blood pressure."

"Killjoy," Gran said, and folded her arms, tucked her head in, and glared ahead of her, the image of a moping child.

"I know how you feel, Gran," said Dooley from the backseat. "We feel just the same way when we have to go see Vena. Isn't that right, Max?"

"Yeah, we don't like to see the doctor either," Max said.

Oh, God, Odelia thought. Sometimes she felt as if she were in charge of a day-care center, not a household of grownups, both cats and humans.

She parked in front of her dad's office and got out. When Gran made no attempt to do the same, she walked around and opened the door. The old lady was still hunched over in her seat, arms folded, a mutinous look on her face.

"Gran, get out."

"I don't wanna."

"Oh, for crying out loud," said Odelia. She unbuckled her grandmother's seatbelt, and physically started dragging the old lady from her seat.

"Hey, this is elder abuse!"

"If you don't start acting like a grownup right now I'll show you elder abuse."

"I'm telling you, I'm not coming!"

For a moment, a tense standoff ensued. A battle of wills.

"I'll go later—right now I want to come with you and solve this murder," said Gran. "I'm fine, okay? I feel great. I'll come with you—we'll interview this Prunella Lemon woman together, and then you can drop me off at Tex's and I'll happily take all the tests you want."

Finally, Odelia relented. "Oh, all right. But only if you promise not to give me a lot of lip if we drop by Dad's later."

Gran mimicked zipping up her lips and Odelia got back into the car.

Gran smiled. "Thanks, honey. I really enjoy sleuthing with you."

"You're just saying that because I gave you what you wanted."

"True," Gran conceded. "But I mean it. I do like sleuthing with my granddaughter."

Odelia suppressed a smile. She wouldn't admit it right now, but she kinda enjoyed her grandmother's company, too. When she wasn't driving her nuts, that is.

CHAPTER 21

"So what's the plan?" I asked as we were back on the road. "Where are we going?"

"First we're going to have a little chat with Prunella Lemon. She's the woman who wrote those Mellie Moose books," said Gran, who appeared to be in a particularly good mood now that danger in the form of a doctor's visit had been averted.

"Ellie Zeus," Odelia corrected her. She directed a critical look at her grandmother. "And then after that I want to have a word with your drug dealer."

"I don't have a drug dealer," said Gran. "I have a supplier of vitamins."

"He's a drug dealer, Gran, and the sooner you admit it the better."

"I will not incriminate myself. He sold me vitamins and until you can prove otherwise I'll believe that's what he sold me. And for a bargain price, too."

"And what do you want us to do?" I asked.

"Talk to anyone you can—try to find out what happened

to Jeb and his ex-wife. I'm sure there will be plenty of pets at the club."

"You say pets, but actually you mean dogs," said Dooley.

"Dogs are pets, too, Dooley," Odelia pointed out.

"I'm not so sure about that," Dooley said quietly as he gave me a look of worry.

"I think it's about time you let go of those ugly prejudices against dogs, boys," said Odelia. "Otherwise you'll never be truly great detectives."

We both howled with indignation. "That's not true!" I cried.

"We don't have anything against dogs!" Dooley said.

"Oh, yes, you do. You don't like dogs, you don't like kittens, you don't like birds. You boys need to widen your horizons. Become a little more tolerant of other species. Imagine if I only talked to women and refused to talk to men? Or only talk to people my age and refuse to talk to kids or the elderly. I wouldn't be much of a detective, would I?"

"That's different and you know it," I said.

"It's not, Max. Dogs are very perceptive, and they spend a lot of time with their humans, maybe even more so than cats, so they're invaluable witnesses. Remember Ringo?"

Ringo was a Chihuahua belonging to a well-known and successful Broadway producer, and had provided us with a telling clue that had solved the murder of Odelia's understudy in a recent Bard in the Park production.

"That's different," I said. "Ringo was a nice dog."

"Most dogs are nice. Just give them a chance."

"Most dogs hate cats," Dooley pointed out.

"Just give them the benefit of the doubt, will you? It's what I do every day."

"Me, too," said Gran. "Tolerance, my boys. Tolerance is key in this business. Love all creatures, great and small, and you will go far." She glanced down at her phone. "That jerk

Scarlett Canyon. She's at it again. Just look at that bathing suit. Makes her look like a clown."

Odelia was darting skeptical glances at her grandmother, and I decided to head off another discussion by asking a more important question: "So have you decided what's going to happen to Bim, Bam and Bom? Are you going to keep them?"

"Why? Don't you think it would be fun to add three kittens to the troupe?"

I hate it when humans answer a question with a question. It's not fair.

"Well, I have to admit they've have grown on me," I said.

"Harriet still hates them," said Gran. "She told me so this morning."

"She's the last holdout," I said. "Even Brutus has fallen in love with them."

"I like them, too," said Dooley. "They're really cute and sweet."

"See?" said Odelia. "Life is so much brighter with three kittens in it."

She still hadn't answered my question, and I had a feeling she never would.

"We're here," she said, proving my point.

We'd arrived at one of those big country clubs, where all the rich people seem to flock. Usually there's a golf club attached, and tennis courts, for some outdoor activities. The men often go off golfing while the women pick up a bronzed and handsome tennis coach and pretend to be interested in tennis. Meanwhile, the older generation sips tea and gossips while scarfing down petit fours and macaroons. I was fully expecting to find the place littered with Chihuahuas, Bichon Frisés and Maltese, and my heart was sinking a little. It's one thing to be a detective, but another always having to deal with a cat's natural enemy.

But then I remembered Odelia's words about giving peace a chance or something along those lines, and I pulled myself together. Your true detective can't be too choosy about the company he keeps, or else he'll never succeed in catching those bad guys.

Odelia let us out of the car, which she'd parked herself, without the assistance of a valet, and then Dooley and I were trotting in the direction of the clubhouse, where we hoped to have many fascinating encounters. Or at least that's what I kept telling myself. Odelia has a book on affirmations, and I had a feeling they would come in handy today.

Every day, in every way, I like dogs better and better and better.

Ugh. Who was I kidding?

CHAPTER 22

A woman waved them over and Odelia waved back. She then turned to her grandmother. "Better behave, all right? No nasty comments from you."

Gran looked indignant. "Nasty comments? Who do you take me for?"

Odelia knew exactly who she took her for. Gran had a sharp tongue sometimes, and could rub people the wrong way. She could also be charming, if she wanted to, but that was the problem: very often she simply didn't want to.

Prunella Lemon looked exactly as in the pictures Odelia had seen: very pretty, with sharp features, long auburn hair and dressed in elegant figure-hugging green and strappy sandals. "Hello," she said as she shook the famous writer's hand. "My name is Odelia Poole."

"Hi there," said the writer in a surprisingly deep voice. "So nice to meet you, Odelia." She turned to Gran. "And you must be Odelia's dear old grandmother."

"That's right," said Gran sweetly. "I'm Odelia's beloved old granny and you must be that wonderful and extremely talented woman who wrote my all-time favorite book."

"Oh, I'm so glad you liked it," said Prunella smoothly.

"Oh, I loved it," said Gran, even though Odelia knew for a fact she'd never read it.

"So what is this all about?" asked the writer, taking a seat.

A cup of coffee had been placed in front of her, as well as a plate of petit fours that looked absolutely delicious. It was all Odelia could do not to snatch one up and pop it into her mouth, which was exactly what the writer did at that exact moment. But instead of offering her guests one of the delicious treats as well, she stayed mum, munching down on the delicacy, then licking her fingers for good measure.

"It's about Jeb Pott," said Odelia. "As I've explained to you over the phone, his family has asked me to look into the murder charges and hopefully find a way to refute them."

Prunella leaned back in the white wrought-iron chair and flicked her hair over her shoulder. It gleamed in the early-morning sunlight. From the terrace where they were sitting, they had a good view of the golf course, where people were teeing off and enjoying the game. To their left, the tennis courts were visible in the distance, and shouts of tennis teachers trying to instruct their pupils to correct their back-hand ripped through the air.

Prunella steepled her long slender fingers thoughtfully. "The thing is, I don't really see how I can be of much assistance in this dreadful matter, Miss Poole—Mrs. Poole."

"Muffin. Poole is Odelia's dad's name. My name is Vesta Muffin," said Gran, who, even after all these years, wasn't all that keen on the name her daughter had assumed.

"Mrs. Muffin," the writer acknowledged. "I know Jeb well, of course. I personally selected him to play Florida Stopper." She grimaced, as if in pain. "As you may have heard, it didn't go well. I lost a great deal of money and the world lost a wonderful movie franchise."

"There won't be a sequel to *Chronicles of Zeus*?" Odelia asked.

The writer closed her eyes. "No, there won't be a sequel. I wrote outlines for five movies, but after the fiasco of the first one there won't be a second, or a third or a fourth or a fifth. And I have Jeb Pott to thank for that." She opened her eyes again. "In the middle of our big launch campaign for the first movie, when the studio was gearing up to give it a mighty push, he chose to engage in a mud-slinging contest with his ex-wife, and the media, always happy to focus on a negative instead of a positive story, associated my movie with the Jeb and Camilla circus. The negative buzz was so overpowering that it scared off my target audience: kids and young families. As you can imagine, absolutely nobody wanted to watch a movie starring a notorious wife beater. And phut went my career as a screenwriter. I don't think I'll ever be in the movie business again."

"I'm so sorry," said Odelia, and she meant it. She'd enjoyed the first *Chronicles of Zeus* movie, and had hoped there would be many sequels in the series.

"Where were you two nights ago between three and five, Mrs. Lemon?" asked Gran.

"Prunella, please," said the writer, and laughed. "Oh, aren't you the hard-hitting detective, Mrs. Muffin?"

"I like to be direct," said Gran. "I get better results that way."

"Yes, maybe you're right. Well, I was fast asleep in bed, actually."

"Anyone witness you being fast asleep in bed? A husband, a lover?"

Prunella laughed again. "My, my, you are direct. Yes, my husband was with me. And in spite of the fact that we've been married twenty-five years, I don't think he would cover for me if I happened to decide to murder the star of my flop movie." A tiny wrinkle appeared between her brows. "But I don't understand. I thought Jeb was the murderer. The newspapers all mention how he was found covered in his ex-wife's blood and how he was still clutching the knife?"

"It certainly looks that way," said Odelia. "And the police are satisfied Jeb is Camilla's killer. It's just that his daughter and his ex-wife Helena don't believe the official story and want to conduct a parallel investigation. They think someone is trying to set Jeb up."

"Oh, my," said Prunella, taken aback. "This is a very fascinating story. And who could this person be? Do you have any clues that support this theory?"

"None whatsoever," said Odelia, who didn't want to give Prunella any insight into their line of inquiry. She was, after all, a potential suspect.

"There are a few things that don't add up. Little things," said Gran, "like—ouch!"

Odelia had given her a kick under the table and Gran eyed her furiously.

"Can you think of anyone who would want to do this to Jeb?" asked Odelia.

Prunella, who'd been following the interaction between granddaughter and grandmother with amusement, pursed her lips. "Um, now let me think. Jeb did have his fair share of enemies, of course, especially after letting down a whole lot of people. In fact you might say that the studio hates his guts right now, as they were left scrambling and then went down in a ball of flame. And then there's the actors who played in *Chronicles of Zeus*, whose careers are now in limbo as a consequence of having featured in the biggest turkey of the decade." She displayed a fine smile. "All in all there must be hundreds of people out there who won't shed a tear for Jeb right now. Worse, they're probably very happy that he's in jail for murder, and might feel he got exactly what he deserved."

"You believe he's guilty, don't you?" asked Odelia.

Prunella wavered. "No, actually I don't. Jeb never struck me as a man with a violent temper. He is volatile, of course. A man-child who never grew up. I mean, people talk about the Peter Pan complex as if it's a good thing, but I can assure you it's very hard to have to deal with a movie star who refuses to grow up and acts like a petulant child at every turn."

"Diva behavior," Gran said, nodding.

"Exactly," said Prunella. "And we all tolerated his behavior, hoping he'd put our movie at the top of the box office. But when he failed, that's when the gloves came off."

Odelia nodded. "Do you think someone hates him enough to frame him for murder?"

"Hated him so bad they'd murder Camilla? I guess so." Prunella lobbed another petit four into her mouth. "I don't envy you, though, Miss Poole. To figure out who amongst all of those haters could be behind this? It seems to me you have your work cut out for you."

That, she had, Odelia conceded. She got up and shook the writer's hand. "Thank you so much for your time, Mrs. Lemon—Prunella. And I hope you'll get to make the rest of your movies. I enjoyed the first one tremendously."

Prunella gave her a sad smile. "There won't be any more movies, but thanks for the compliment."

As Odelia and Gran turned away, suddenly Gran gasped, "Oh, no, you don't!" then stalked off. And when Odelia looked up, she saw she was making a beeline for Scarlett Canyon, who sat holding court on the other side of the terrace.

Oh, no. Exactly what they needed right now. Not!

CHAPTER 23

As usual, Scarlett was surrounded by a huddle of male admirers. Odelia had to hand it to her: even though she was Gran's age, she still looked stunning. Even though she owed a lot to her plastic surgeon: her lips were ridiculously plump and her chest outrageously pumped up. As usual, she'd squeezed herself into a skimpy dress a few sizes too small.

"What do you think you're doing?" asked Gran as she approached.

"I'm sure I don't know what you're talking about," said Scarlett, tilting her chin.

Gran took out her phone. "This is what I'm talking about. You've started a flog."

"So? People start vlogs all the time. Why not me?"

"Only you called your flog the Sly Sleuth!"

"Pretty clever, don't you think? I'm very proud of it."

"You copied my name! *My* flog is called the Sly Sleuth!"

"Oh, I'm sure that's just a coincidence, Vesta, dear."

"And you're covering the exact same topics I am!"

Scarlett studied her talon-like pink nails. "Well, some

things are simply eternal bestsellers. Or did you really think you had the monopoly on crime vlogging?"

"You're a liar and a cheat and a fraud," Gran snapped. "And you're going to take down that flog right this second!"

Scarlett threw her head back, a mass of copper-colored curls dangling as she let rip a hearty laugh. Her small group of male admirers all laughed along pleasantly. They probably had no idea what was going on but they seemed to enjoy themselves tremendously.

"Gran, you're making a scene," Odelia told her grandmother. All eyes on the terrace had swiveled in their direction, and even Prunella Lemon sat drinking in the tawdry scene with relish. She was probably taking notes to use in one of her bestselling novels later on.

"Oh, Vesta dear, you're so funny when you're angry," said Scarlett, fixing her cat-like eyes on Gran. "There is no copyright in the vlogging sphere. None whatsoever. If I want to name my vlog exactly like yours, there's not a thing you can do about it. Not one thing."

"We'll see about that," grunted Gran. "I'll write to Mr. Google right now, and ask him to—"

"Mr. Google!" Scarlett laughed. "That's so precious!"

"We'll see who's laughing after Mr. Google removes your flog and upholds mine as the one and only true original Sly Sleuth."

"Well, you do what you have to, my darling," said Scarlett. "And when you write to your Mr. Google, don't forget to tell him you're his number one flogger." She giggled at that.

"Let's go, Gran," said Odelia, taking her grandmother's arm. "She's not worth your time."

"No, she's not," Gran agreed.

"Still writing your silly little articles, Odelia, dear?" asked Scarlett.

"Still sponging off rich bachelors, Scarlett, dear?" Odelia returned.

This didn't sit well with the woman, for her smile vanished. "Better show some respect to your Auntie Scarlett," she snapped, her eyes flashing dangerously. "I've known your family for a long time. I know where all the bodies are buried. And if I wanted to, I could spill all your dirty little secrets on my vlog."

"Oh, just go away, Scarlett," said Odelia, and walked off, joining her grandmother who'd taken a stool at the bar.

"The nerve of that woman," Gran grumbled.

"You know she's just doing this to get a rise out of you, don't you?" said Odelia, as she held up her hand to attract the bartender's attention. She ordered a cup of chamomile tea for her grandmother, hoping it would calm her down, and a Diet Coke for herself.

"I know that," said Gran. "Of course I know that. But the woman is pure evil. I just can't let her get away with it."

"And you do know that the person who runs Google isn't called Mr. Google, right?"

This seemed to surprise Gran. "Google isn't named after its owner?"

"No, it's not, just like Instagram isn't named after its owner, or Facebook."

"Well, I knew Amazon wasn't named after Jeff Bezos," Gran conceded. "I just figured Mr. Google had started his search engine from his garage, just like Bill Microsoft and that nice young Steve Apple."

"It's Bill Gates and Steve Jobs, and there is no Mr. Google."

"Too bad," said Gran, slumping in her chair.

It was those ecstasy pills, Odelia knew. First they lifted you up to the highest heights, then slammed you down into the lowest lows. And now Gran was experiencing those lows very keenly, especially after discovering that Scarlett had plagiarized her precious vlog.

From the corner of her eye, Odelia saw Max and Dooley sneaking across the terrace, in search of pets to talk to. She smiled. At least they might yield some results. So far she had nothing to show for her work. Just then, Prunella joined them at the bar, accompanied by a handsome man in his fifties, sporting a full head of white hair.

"Miss Poole, Mrs. Muffin," said Prunella, "this is my husband Charlie. Charlie, these are the detectives Fae Pott hired to clear her father's name." She turned to Odelia. "I remembered something just now. The person who really has it in for Jeb is Fitz Priestley. And you'll find that he lives next to where Jeb is staying." She gestured with her head to a man seated three tables away, holding court to a captive audience of young men and women. "If you want to ask him a few questions, he's right there." She nudged her husband.

"Right," he muttered, then plastered an appealing smile on his bronzed face. He clearly had been spending a lot of time in the Hamptons, even though his accent revealed he was an Englishman through and through. "While Jeb Pott was busy butchering his ex-wife, Prunella was next to me, fast asleep in bed. So even though she might have wanted to frame Jeb for murder by taking a big old whack at his ex, she didn't, is what I'm trying to say."

"Oh, Charlie, please don't be so crass."

"What did I say?"

"These people believe Jeb is innocent."

He raised his eyebrows in surprise. "They do? How quaint."

"Yes, it is," said Prunella, "but there you have it."

"Jeb is a raving lunatic and a deeply unpleasant human being," said Charlie, turning serious. "This murder business? It was only a matter of time before the man snapped and turned homicidal. I'm glad he's in prison right now, exactly where the little turd belongs."

"You really think Jeb is capable of murder?"

"Of course. With the mountains of coke the freak snorted, and who knows what stuff he injected into his veins, it doesn't surprise me he turned completely whacko at some point. There's only so much the human body can take before it goes completely haywire."

"Charlie is a doctor," said Prunella with an affectionate smile. "He's the one who warned me not to hire Jeb for my project, but of course I wouldn't listen."

"I knew the movie was sunk the moment we had our first meeting with Jeb and the director," said Charlie, who'd hooked his thumbs into his waistcoat.

"I'd asked Charlie to be present at the meeting," Prunella explained. "For moral support. It was my first big Hollywood project and I was incredibly nervous, you see."

"One look at Jeb and I knew he was a ticking time bomb just waiting to go off," Charlie said. "The shifty eyes, the affectated speech, those weird mannerisms. I could tell the man was an addict. And drug addicts don't make for the most stable people to work with."

"Such a pity," Prunella murmured. "He was so handsome and so talented as a young man. And look at him now..."

She moved away, followed by her husband, and Odelia saw that Gran had slumped even more on her barstool and was practically falling down from the thing.

"Here, drink your tea," she said, pushing the cup in front of her.

"I don't wanna," Gran muttered, resting her head on her arms on top of the bar.

"Drink your tea while I go talk to Fitz Priestley," she ordered.

"Wait. I'll join you," said Gran, but she looked so worn out there was no way she was going to be of much help now. "I need another vitamin," she muttered, her eyes drooping closed. "Just another vitamin. A, B, C, D, E, F, G… Any vitamin will do."

"No more vitamins for you, Gran. At least not the kind you've been popping."

She moved over to where Fitz Priestley was sitting and introduced herself. He gave her a quick glance, then dismissed her with a wave of the hand. "I'm sorry," he said. "I'm afraid I don't have time for amateur sleuths. Now get lost, Miss Poole, before I call security."

Blushing scarlet at being dismissed so rudely, Odelia gritted her teeth. "Listen to me, buster. Jeb Pott's daughter hired me to prove her dad's innocence, and you're going to talk to me or else I'll write in tomorrow's Hampton Cove Gazette that you're the rudest, nastiest, most obnoxious director ever to set foot in this town. You got that?"

A slow grin spread across his narrow face. "My god, woman," he exclaimed. "Have you considered working in Hollywood? You'd be a perfect fit!" He then gestured to a chair. "Here, take a seat. And tell me all about Jeb Pott and his remarkable wealth of problems."

CHAPTER 24

As Dooley and I searched around for a sign of canine activity, we found ourselves faced with a unique problem: there was a distinct dearth of dogs in this exclusive club. We'd already been there ten minutes, and Odelia and Gran had probably finished their interview, and we still hadn't been able to find a single dog.

"This is so weird," I told Dooley. "It's almost as if dogs aren't allowed on the premises."

"Maybe they aren't," Dooley said. "I've heard of places where pets are not allowed. There are even landlords that forbid them. Can you believe that?"

I told him I most certainly could. "Not all humans are like Odelia, Dooley," I said. "Not all of them love pets the way she does."

"Hard to imagine," said Dooley as he sniffed the air. Dogs have a very particular and distinctive odor, and it's not hard to pick up the trace. Only at this very moment neither of us could detect a single canine anywhere in the vicinity. Not a one.

And we'd finished our sweep of the terrace and were

about to take in the tennis courts, hoping to have more luck there, when suddenly we ourselves were swept up, and not in a good way either.

"Hey!" I cried when a strong hand grabbed me by the neck and hoisted me into the air. "What's the big idea?!"

"No cats allowed, I'm afraid," a grating voice announced.

I turned my head to take in the miscreant who was cathandling us and saw that it was a large man with a round head and a weird little goatee beard.

"Rules are rules," he then said, and took a firmer grip on the both of us and carried us away.

"Hey! Odelia! Odelia!" I cried, but she was too far and my cries were in vain.

"Max, we're being catnapped," said Dooley, sounding scared and confused.

One would feel scared and confused for less.

"He's just throwing us out," I said. "No need to worry. He'll carry us to the front gate and kick us out of his club. No big deal."

"Yeah, but what if he doesn't? What if he hands us over to the chef and he puts us in today's stew?!"

The prospect of ending up in the meat grinder made me gulp a bit. On top of that I was experiencing a certain amount of discomfort. It's not much fun being carried by the scruff of the neck when you are a kitten, but even less when you're a full-bodied cat that weighs closer to twenty pounds than ten. I experienced a certain pulling sensation at the nape of the neck that was distinctly painful and extremely unpleasant.

"Just let us down, will you, fellow?" I asked. "We got the message. We'll just walk out the door and you'll never see us again."

"Rules are rules," the big guy repeated, as if he were a broken record.

"Yeah, I know rules are rules, and I'm sorry we broke them, but this is not the way to treat a valued member of the community. And trust me, we are both very valued members of this community, feline or otherwise."

"Yeah, we've solved a lot of mysteries together, and our owner is none other than the famous Odelia Poole," said Dooley.

"She's a reporter," I added, "and if you don't put us down right now she's going to write a pretty nasty piece about you and your club."

All to no avail, of course. The guy wasn't going to let us go before he'd hand-delivered us to the front gate—or, as in Dooley's nightmarish scenario, to the kitchen chef.

"Rules are there for a reason," the guy muttered. "And when rules are broken, there are consequences."

I just hoped those consequences didn't involve being turned into fricassee.

He carried us to a door, then deposited us into a small cage and locked it carefully.

"Max, I don't like this," Dooley announced.

"I don't like it either, Dooley," I intimated.

He then placed the cage in the back of a golf cart, got behind the wheel, and pushed a button. The thing came to life with a soft purr and then we were off, Dooley and I locked up in the cage, being carted off in a direction unknown, by a man who seemed to love rules.

We rode through a landscape that looked like the golf course part of the country club, and I wondered if he was going to give us golfing lessons next. I didn't think so. That probably wasn't in his particular rulebook.

Just then, a booming voice had us both jump up to the top of our cage.

"Sad day," boomed the voice.

CHAPTER 25

We turned in the direction of the voice, and found ourselves looking at a second cage, placed next to ours. This one was bigger, and contained a sad-looking Droopy dog.

We'd finally found our dog. Though perhaps not in the most pleasant of circumstances.

"Oh, hey, dog," I said by way of greeting. "My name is Max, and this is Dooley."

"Melvin," said the Basset Hound. "So they caught you guys trespassing too, huh?"

"We weren't trespassing," I said with a measure of indignation. "Our human didn't know this place had rules about pets, so she brought us along in her car."

"I was just looking for a bite to eat," said the sad dog in a drawling voice. "And each time I come to this club I get to have a nice gourmet meal. Unless I'm caught and kicked out, of course," he added mournfully.

From his demeanor I guessed he hadn't had time to enjoy his gourmet meal before being kicked out today, though.

"So what are you cats doing here?" he asked.

"Our human is a detective. She solves murders," I explained. "And right now she's trying to solve the murder of Camilla Kirby."

"So she brought us here hoping to talk to someone who knows Jeb Pott—that's Camilla's ex-husband—and shed some light on this murder business," Dooley continued.

"I know Jeb," said the dog.

I was surprised by this. "You do?"

"Oh, sure. We used to spend a lot of time together."

I couldn't believe our luck. Of all the places in town, we'd found the one place where we got to meet Jeb Pott's dog.

"So Jeb is your human, huh?"

"Oh, no. I don't have a human. I belong to no one. Well," he corrected himself after a pause, "I used to belong to someone, but that was before they tied me to a tree and took off. I haven't belonged to anyone since."

"What a horrible thing to do!" Dooley said. "Who does that?"

"Humans," said the dog. "That's who."

"Not all humans are like that," I told the dog. "Our human would never, ever do such a horrible, unspeakable thing."

"Yeah, yeah," he said, clearly not giving much credence to my words. "So Jeb, huh? Long time no see. We used to have such a good time when he was in town. He'd stumble from bar to bar and I'd follow him, then when he was passed out on the street, drunk as a skunk, I'd keep him company. People would pass us by and throw money in his hat, and a bone for me. I ate the bones, and Jeb, when he finally woke up from his drunken stupor, would use the money to buy us a nice meal. A burger for him, and a nice sausage for me."

"Did this... happen fairly recently?" I asked, surprised that a Hollywood megastar would choose to live the life of a common tramp.

"Oh, sure. Only last month we went on another one of

our midnight benders. Well, he went on his bender, while I stuck close to him and made sure he arrived home safe and sound. Jeb has balance issues, and orientation issues, and... Well, a lot of issues, I guess."

"Jeb supposedly killed his ex-wife two nights ago," I said. "So now we're trying to find out if he really did kill her, or if maybe somebody else did and they're trying to blame him."

"Jeb would never kill anyone," said Melvin decidedly. "Jeb is a dog lover, and dog lovers are not killers."

"Yes, but he really didn't like his ex-wife, and maybe he finally decided that enough was enough and so he killed her in a rage."

"Not a rage," Dooley said. "He invited her by text, so he must have planned it."

"Premeditated murder," said Melvin, nodding. He seemed to be a dog of the world. "No, Jeb doesn't have it in him to do such a thing. Take my word for it, cats. I've seen him give his last cent to a street bum."

From one street bum to another, I thought. It didn't mean that Jeb wouldn't kill Camilla, of course. It's not because someone loves dogs and bums that he doesn't harbor a festering hatred towards the woman he blames for his downfall.

"If anyone did this, it's one of the guys Jeb owes money to," said Melvin.

"Jeb owes money?" I asked, surprised.

"I thought he was rich," said Dooley. "Aren't all Hollywood stars filthy rich?"

"Not all of them," I said. And apparently Jeb lost a lot of money in the divorce. Lawyers are costly, and so are ex-wives with expensive tastes.

"This happened six weeks ago," said Melvin. "We'd just been kicked out of a bar and Jeb and I were lying next to a dumpster in some back alley, Jeb counting his few remaining greenbacks while I was counting my blessings for having found a piece of pepperoni pizza someone had carelessly discarded, when five men walked into the alley, armed with baseball bats. They were looking for Jeb. The leader of the pack had a scar that ran all the way from his right eye to the corner of his mouth, and a tattoo of a scorpion on the side of his neck. Jeb called him Cicero, and they obviously knew each other well.

"Cicero then said that if Jeb didn't pay back what he owed, he was going to take the bat to his kneecaps, which would have caused Jeb considerable pain, not to mention trouble in his career as an actor. Not many actors can act with two broken kneecaps, obviously."

"Obviously," I agreed.

"So Jeb said he was going to get him the money. He said he was selling one of his houses in LA and once the deal was done he'd pay back every cent he owed. Cicero then struck Jeb across the jaw for good measure, and Jeb laughed, saying it was an honor to be beaten up by the famous Cicero. He said to give his regards to Animal, Cicero's boss."

"Animal?" asked Dooley. "Cicero's boss is an animal?"

"I think he's a human who calls himself Animal," Melvin explained.

"Weird," Dooley said, and I agreed with him. Like an animal calling itself Human.

"And what happened next?" I asked, fascinated by this rare glimpse into Hampton Cove's criminal underbelly.

"Nothing. Cicero and his crew left, and Jeb started belting out a song about cigarettes and alcohol. He seemed to enjoy himself tremendously, and announced he'd carry the scar Cicero had given him like a badge of honor. I could tell there was a hidden sadness lurking underneath his surface gaiety, though," he added, suddenly becoming philosophical.

"So you think this Cicero or his boss Animal could have

killed Camilla Kirby and put the blame squarely on Jeb?" I asked.

"Possible," Melvin said. "Or he could have decided to murder Jeb and once he arrived changed his mind and murdered Camilla instead. Humans are fickle like that."

"They are," I agreed. The story certainly had the ring of truth to it, though it was hard to imagine a rich megastar like Jeb Pott having to borrow money from a notorious gangster. Then again, from what I'd heard it was obvious Jeb had recently fallen on hard times.

The golf cart suddenly came to an abrupt halt and Dooley, Melvin and I were flung against the front of our respective cages. Then the man dismounted the vehicle and opened first our cage, then Melvin's. He then escorted us towards the front gate of the club and waited patiently until we'd walked out through the gate.

"Rules are rules," he told us apologetically. "Nothing personal. But rules are—"

"Rules, yes, we get it," I said, starting to see that this was a man with one of those one-track minds you always hear so much about.

"Well, I gotta be going," said Melvin as soon as the man had closed the front gate on us. "Other country clubs to hit, other dumpsters to examine."

"Listen," I said as he started to walk away.

He glanced over his shoulder. "What?"

"If you ever want to enjoy a great meal, you can visit us at our place."

"Yeah," said Dooley. "You're always welcome, Melvin. We have a very nice human who'll treat you right. And I wouldn't be surprised if she threw in a nice bath, too."

Melvin frowned. "Are you telling me I stink, cat?"

"Oh, no!" Dooley was quick to say. "Not at all!"

"Just... making you an offer," I said. "An offer you can

refuse if you want to, of course. But a nice bath and a bowl full of food are waiting for you if you want."

The dog's expression softened. "Thanks," he said. "Maybe one of these days I'll take you up on that offer. See ya, boys."

"See ya, Melvin," we said, and watched him trudge off in the direction of the road.

"So now what?" said Dooley.

"Now we wait for Odelia to come driving through that gate."

Flanking the gate were two large statues of lions. It seemed apt, so we each climbed one, stretched out on top, and waited. Cats are great waiters. In fact we can wait for hours. It's that hunting instinct, honed for millions and millions of years. And then we promptly fell asleep. What? You try being a jungle gym to three kittens. You'd be exhausted, too.

CHAPTER 26

"So Fae hired you, huh?" said Fitz Priestley with a chuckle. He'd sent his admirers away to practice their sycophancy elsewhere, and now it was just him and Odelia. "She always was a very enterprising young woman."

"You know her?"

"Of course. I know the whole family. Jeb and I go way back. We were neighbors for years. This was obviously before he divorced his lovely wife and left her for that starlet."

"Camilla Kirby."

The director nodded.

He took off his fashionable gold-rimmed sunglasses and polished them on the hem of his shirt. He was dressed eclectically, with a sleeveless pink silk shirt, gold-embroidered waistcoat and his hair shaved above his ears and standing up like a rooster's comb. Not unlike Jeb's style of dress, even though the director was the actor's senior by a decade.

"I always considered Jeb a member of my family. Our daughters are the same age, and Fae and Lucy have been best friends for years, as are my wife Suzy and Helena."

"It is rumored that you and Jeb had a falling-out, though. Is that true?"

He fixed her with a bleary eye. "Privacy is dead, isn't it? Have a fight with your best friend and the whole world sticks its nose in. Tell me, Miss Poole. If you and your best friend quarrel, would you enjoy reading about it in the *New York Post* or the *National Enquirer*? I don't think so. But I had to read all about my tiff with Jeb. Every last detail. And the only person who could have supplied those details was me or Jeb, as we'd been the only ones present. And since I never breathed a word about it to anyone, the conclusion is obvious."

"Jeb could have told a friend, who could have told a reporter."

"You're right," he conceded. "And I know I should have talked to Jeb before jumping to conclusions. Still, it wasn't a nice surprise to read my own words, spoken in anger, plastered all across the *National Enquirer's* front page in big, bold lettering."

"The fight was about Jeb's divorce?"

"Yes, it was. I thought he was being a damn fool to leave Helena for a treacherous gold-digging bimbo like Camilla Kirby. It was obvious to me—in fact it was obvious to anyone but Jeb himself—that the only thing Miss Kirby was interested in was the raised profile marriage to a mega-star like Jeb would bring. Once that was accomplished, she dropped Jeb like a hot potato. Now she was playing leads in global blockbusters whereas before she was only known to a handful of people in the industry, featuring in indie movies and making no money. So mission accomplished, I would say, except for Jeb, because he has now become a pariah, his career a shambles, his present a pitiful afterthought to an otherwise stellar past."

"Why did Camilla destroy Jeb's career? Or is it possible he really was abusive to her?"

"I don't think so. Of course, it's very difficult for an outsider to know what goes on inside a marriage, but Jeb is not a violent man. He's prone to temper tantrums, but he'll never take them out on anyone. He'll close up like a clam and retreat from the world. At heart he's a benign soul and I don't recognize him in the stories that have been written about him."

"Only now he's being accused of having murdered Camilla."

"Impossible," said the director. "Jeb? Murder? Out of the question. There must be some other explanation. And that's where you come in, don't you, Miss Poole?"

"The police are convinced he did it, though."

"Yes, well, the police are not infallible. The truth will out, and when it does, I'm one hundred percent certain it will exonerate Jeb completely."

"Some people say that you might be the one behind this whole plot to implicate Jeb," she said. "What do you have to say to that?"

He laughed. "Priceless!" He pressed a hand to his chest. "Me? A murderer? Absolutely priceless. Who told you this?"

She shrugged.

"Why would I ever want to hurt Miss Kirby? Or Jeb, for that matter?"

"Because Jeb didn't just wreck his own career when he divorced Camilla, but yours as well. Your last high-profile project was three years ago, an eternity in Hollywood. And as far as I can tell there's nothing on your slate. So it's not just Jeb who's been turned into a pariah in his own industry. The same goes for you, Mr. Priestley."

He stared at her for a moment, his jaw working. It was obvious she'd touched a raw nerve. "Myes," he said finally. "It is true that Jeb's tribulations reflect badly on me, as he's always been what some people would call my muse. But Jeb doesn't define my career. I'm still the one in charge of my own destiny. Directors have had muses and then replaced them with others. Martin Scorsese replaced Robert De Niro with Leonardo DiCaprio. Alfred Hitchcock exchanged Grace Kelly with Tippi Hedren... I'll survive this temporary setback."

"I hope you do. I really enjoy your movies, Mr. Priestley."

He flashed a quick and rare smile. "Thank you. That's nice to hear. At any rate, the fact that I haven't had a movie made in three years is not entirely Jeb's fault. I'm as much to blame as he is. The fact of the matter is that my wife has been facing some health issues lately, and they've demanded my full attention."

"I'm sorry to hear that."

He leaned forward. "Please don't print any of this, Miss Poole. Yes, I know you're a reporter as well as an amateur sleuth. Which explains my outburst earlier. I'm not the media's biggest fan right now. And this is all strictly private. So if you print a word of this..."

"I won't write a word. I promise," she said quickly. And she wouldn't. She was a reporter with a strict ethical code of conduct, as was her boss Dan.

"Yes, Gail has cancer. Ovarian cancer. She's fighting hard, but the prospects are not good. Not good at all. We're taking her to Switzerland next week, for an experimental treatment. So you see, my mind is not on movies right now. And as luck would have it, I have made enough money over the past thirty years that I can afford to retire and devote this time to my beloved wife." He stared into the distance for a moment, where old men were still hitting little white balls then chasing after them. He heaved a deep sigh. "At any rate, it's very good of you to take Jeb's case to heart. Even though I've been extremely upset with him, he doesn't deserve to be punished for a crime he didn't commit."

"Why don't you tell him so yourself?" she suggested. "Maybe now is a good time to make your peace with each other."

He gave her a weak smile. "Reporter, sleuth and confessor. You are a special lady, Miss Poole."

She would have added cat lady, but didn't. There were certain secrets the world had no business knowing. She certainly agreed with the director on that. And as she took her leave, she placed a hand on his shoulder and he gave her a nod of appreciation. She now realized all his bluster was simply a front to hide the pain he was experiencing. Pain he couldn't share with anyone because of his position in the industry and his fame.

"Poor man," she said as she returned to her barstool.

Gran didn't respond. She'd fallen asleep where she sat.

She gently shook her and finally Gran stirred, licking her lips. "It wasn't me, Dr. Franklin. Nurse Jackson stole that diamond." She blinked when she realized where she was. "Weird," she said. "I must have dozed off."

"We need to get you home," said Odelia. "Come on. Let's go."

"I'm not going home," said Gran. "I'm going to interview more suspects and solve this mystery."

But as Odelia put her grandmother in the car and buckled her up, the old lady promptly fell asleep again.

Ecstasy, thought Odelia. They should probably change the name to misery instead.

She drove back to the entrance, and then through it and out. And as she did, she happened to glance in her rearview mirror and who should she see there but Max and Dooley, fast asleep atop two lions!

CHAPTER 27

We were driving through town, Grandma asleep next to Odelia, and Dooley asleep next to me. The only ones still standing—so to speak—were Odelia and me.

"Where are we going?" I asked, yawning.

"My dad's," Odelia said, looking grim. She cut a quick glance to her grandmother, who was out like a light. "I don't like this, Max. Maybe we should take her to a hospital."

"Tex will know what to do."

Just then, Gran suddenly sprang to life again. "Yes, your highness, I'm just a lonely virgin from Iowa lost in the woods!" She glanced around. "Where am I?"

"In my car. I'm taking you to see my dad."

"Oh, do I have to?" asked Gran in a whiny voice. "You know I hate doctors."

"You work for one."

"That doesn't mean I can't hate them," she said reasonably.

"You promised you wouldn't fight me on this, remember?"

"Oh, all right. Have it your way," said Gran, slumping down in her seat again. "But he won't find a thing. I'm as fit as a baby kangaroo." Just then she spotted something through the windshield. "There! It's Conrad!"

"Your drug dealer?"

"My vitamin supplier," Gran corrected her. "Pull over. I'm going to ask him a straight question and he's going to give me a straight answer and you'll see that he's an honest vitamin salesman and not a nasty drug dealer as you keep implying."

"Deal," said Odelia, and pulled the car over to the side of the road.

We were on the outskirts of Hampton Cove, in one of the more residential areas. Mostly families with kids lived there, and I wondered what a drug dealer would be doing in a nice neighborhood like this. Unless he really was a vitamin salesman, of course. We can all use some extra vitamins from time to time.

"Hey, you!" Odelia bellowed the moment she'd cut the engine and cranked down the window. "Conrad, right?"

The guy grinned broadly at the mention of his name and came walking over. He'd been leaning against his own vehicle, a spiffy new Toyota Land Cruiser, and was dressed in cowboy boots, skinny jeans, a fringed red cowboy shirt and a wide-brimmed cowboy hat. In Texas, he would have fit right in. In Hampton Cove he stuck out like a sore thumb.

"Howdy," he said, tipping his hat. "What can I do you for, little lady?"

"Howdy!" Gran yelled from the other side of the car, and dipped her head down to show her face to the man.

His smile widened. "Mrs. Muffin! My best customer! Don't tell me you ran out already!"

"My granddaughter here confiscated my stash, that's what the problem is. She won't believe me when I tell her you've been selling me vitamins and nothing but vitamins. She claims you've sold me ecstasy—whatever the hell that is—and she doesn't like it."

The man's smile faltered. "Um, yeah. No, of course I sold you vitamins. You came to me for a pick-me-up so that's what I gave you."

"So if I take these to the police and have them examined at the police lab," said Odelia, holding up her grandmother's pills, "they'll clearly show up as vitamin pills, right?"

His eyes went little wider, and a lot wilder. "Police?" He stepped back from the vehicle. "Now, little lady, why would you go and do a thing like that? I'm just an honest businessman, trying to make an honest buck here."

"You didn't answer my question. If I give these pills to my uncle—who happens to be chief of police in this here town of ours—"

"And my son," said Grandma."

"—and he has them examined—"

"You never told me your son was chief of police!" the guy yelled.

Next to me, Dooley stirred. "What's going on? What's with all the yelling?"

"Odelia is busting this drug dealer's chops and he doesn't like it," I said, giving him the CliffsNotes version of events.

"Does it make a difference?" asked Odelia. "If you sold my grandmother vitamins that's perfectly fine. But if you sold her ecstasy, on the other hand..."

The cowboy wannabe was backtracking in the direction of his car now. "I think you better leave now, lady. I'm not doing business with you—nor you, Mrs. Muffin."

"Hey, what about my vitamins?" asked Gran, getting a little worked up.

"I'm fresh out!" said the guy, waving his hands. "Got nothing left, I'm sorry!"

He then got into his car and slammed the door.

Odelia gave her gran a questioning look, then Gran said, "Hit it," and Odelia hit it.

I had no idea what she was supposed to hit, but as it turned out, it was the gas. She'd put the car in reverse, and now stomped her foot on the accelerator. And even as the drug dealer tried to maneuver his car out of the parking spot he'd squeezed it in, she hit him in the front fender with a crunching sound of iron grinding against iron.

"Hey!" the guy yelled, sticking his head out the window. "This is a new car!"

Odelia slammed the car in gear again, moved a few inches to the front, then reversed into the Toyota once more, hitting it with such force something came loose and dropped down on the ground.

"My car!" the guy screamed, and when I looked back, he was on the verge of tears.

"That's what you get for selling drugs to old ladies!" Odelia yelled, and then pushed so hard on the gas that Conrad's car was shoved backward and into the car behind him, now effectively boxed in with nowhere to go.

He must have understood what she was trying to accomplish, for he opened the door and started to make a run for it. But Odelia is a much better runner than any drug dealer, and she caught him in no time, tackled him to the tarmac, then straddled him.

"Gran! Call Alec!" she yelled.

"Already on it!" Gran yelled back, taking out her phone.

"This is a free country!" the guy cried as he squirmed helplessly. "Free enterprise is the backbone of America!"

"Not when you're dealing dope," said Odelia.

Moments later, the cavalry arrived in the form of Uncle Alec. When the guy saw him, he knew the jig was up and dropped his head on the asphalt, losing the cowboy hat.

"Ugh," he said.

"This man has been selling drugs to senior citizens, convincing them they were vitamins," said Odelia, getting up.

"And do we know any of these senior citizens?" asked Alec with a twinkle in his eye.

Gran threw up her hands. "He told me they were vitamins!"

Alec sighed. "Conrad Jenkins," he said, helping the man up. "You're under arrest."

"Fine," said the guy. "I'll never sell dope to your mom again. Now can I go?"

"You wish," grunted Alec, taking off his sunglasses and tucking them away. "Now what have I told you about selling dope in my town?"

"Um... not to do it?"

"Exactly. Last time you got off easy. This time I'm throwing the book at you, buddy. And hopefully this time the lesson will stick."

"Hey, I'm just a businessman."

"You're a dope peddler, and you were trying to tap a new market by selling your poison to kids." He gestured to the school located at the end of the street.

So that's what he was doing there. Bad man, I thought. Very bad man.

"Before you take him in," said Odelia, "can I have a quick word?"

"You can have all the words you want, honey," said Alec. "I'm grateful you got this piece of crap off my streets. Again," he added, getting into the guy's face.

"Yeah, yeah," said Conrad. "Don't rub it in."

Odelia moved a few feet away from her uncle.

"So what is it you want to know?" asked Conrad wearily.

"Jeb Pott. He's one of your customers, isn't he?"

The guy studied her for a moment, then smiled, displaying a row of perfectly even and blindingly white teeth.

"The drug trade must be a very lucrative one," said Dooley, "if he can afford nice snappers like that."

"I guess so," I said, following the back-and-forth between Odelia and Conrad intently.

"What is this information worth to you?" asked the guy now.

"Listen, buster. You poisoned my grandmother. So don't push me."

"All right, all right," he said, his smile vanishing. "Okay, yeah, I was Jeb's dealer when he was in town. And a great client he was, too. Pretty much bought up my entire supply of whatever I had to offer. Mary Jane, boom, smack, gum, snow, bennies, ice, uppers, rope, goop, K, angel dust, magic mint, Robo, blue heaven, cactus, shrooms, poppers, uppers..."

I shared a look with Dooley and shook my head. He shook his, too.

"So he paid you?" asked Odelia, unfazed. "No debts?"

"Hey, what do I look like to you? A banker? I don't do credit, all right? You want the stuff, you pay cash on delivery."

"Ask him if he's ever heard of a guy called Animal," I said. "Or Cicero."

"Do the names Animal or Cicero mean anything to you?" asked Odelia.

The man's face instantly displayed an expression of fear. "I got nothing to do with those guys. Nothing whatsoever. They stay out of my way, and I stay out of theirs."

"Jeb was deeply in debt with this Animal person," I said. "And Cicero, who works for Animal, threatened to break Jeb's kneecaps with a baseball bat if he didn't pay up."

"Is it possible Jeb borrowed money from this Animal to buy your merchandise?" asked Odelia.

The guy shrugged. "It's possible. But not likely. I mean, this is Jeb Pott we're talking about. World-famous actor? The guy must be loaded, right? Private jet, condo in Manhattan, mansion in the Hamptons, yacht in the South of France, private island in the Caribbean. Vacation home in Gstaad. Why would he borrow money from the Animal?"

Odelia nodded, then glanced down at me. "Apparently that's exactly what he did."

"If he did, that was very stupid of him," said Conrad. "And if he didn't pay, he's a dead man."

Uncle Alec put Conrad into his squad car and read him his rights.

Odelia crouched down next to me. "So tell me more about this Animal." I told her the story about meeting Melvin, and she smiled. "See? I told you dogs are nice." She tickled my chin. "You need to keep an open mind in this business, Max. Otherwise you won't get far."

"Lesson learned," I said. "So are you going to talk to this Mr. Animal now?"

"Not right now. I'm taking Gran to my dad first. If she's been popping ecstasy she needs a full medical." She shook her head as she got up. "What the heck was she thinking?"

"I was thinking I was buying vitamins!" Gran yelled from the car. "Vitamins!"

CHAPTER 28

Arriving at her dad's, Odelia helped her grandmother out of the car, but Gran quickly slapped her arm away. "I'm not an invalid," she snapped.

"I know, I know. Just be careful where you step, all right?"

Gran grumbled something under the breath that didn't sound like the kind of thing one should say to one's beloved granddaughter, then sailed into the doctor's office under her own steam. She stepped inside and Odelia followed right behind. In the waiting room only one patient sat. It was Mrs. Baumgartner, Dad's least favorite but most loyal patient. Not a week went by that Mrs. Baumgartner didn't set foot in the office at least once.

A bluff, apple-cheeked and heavyset middle-aged lady, she was probably the healthiest person in Hampton Cove, which hadn't stopped her from suffering a long list of ailments, all of them gleaned from Wikipedia and the medical encyclopedias she collected.

"Hey, Ida," Gran grumbled.

"Oh, hello there, Vesta," said Mrs. Baumgartner. She checked her watch.

Gran got the message. "I'm not here to work. I'm here to see the doctor."

"Ooh, are you sick? You certainly look sick—in fact you look terrible."

Gran's eyes shot three sheets of flame in Mrs. Baumgartner's direction, who quickly shut up.

"I'm not sick," Gran said emphatically. "It's Odelia. She's got this obsession that there must be something wrong with me, even though I keep telling her I'm perfectly fine."

"Do you mind if we cut in, Mrs. Baumgartner?" asked Odelia.

"Oh, no, I don't mind at all. In fact I've got all the time in the world."

When the door to the inner office opened and Odelia's dad appeared, he looked surprised to see his daughter and mother-in-law. "Odelia? Vesta? Is something the matter?"

"No," said Gran.

"Yes," said Odelia.

An elderly man Odelia recognized as Mr. Soot came shuffling out, pressed Dad's hand warmly, and shuffled on out the door.

"Come on in," said Dad, and ushered the both of them into his office.

"Get well soon, Vesta!" Mrs. Baumgartner yelled before the door closed. "We miss you!"

When Gran was assisting Odelia on her investigations, there was no one to staff the reception at the doctor's office, so Dad had to work a little harder to answer all the phones. It was one of the reasons Odelia preferred to do these murder inquires by herself. She knew Dad didn't mind, but she also knew he preferred to have Gran taking care of the front desk, and contend with the patients. The fact of the matter was that Gran liked the change of pace. She didn't enjoy being cooped up in the office all day and looked forward to these trips with her granddaughter, interviewing suspects and catching killers. It provided her with the kind of excitement and thrills life as a doctor's assistant lacked.

"So? What's going on?" asked Dad, a good-natured man with a shock of white hair and the bedside manner of a country doctor.

"Nothing," said Gran.

"Everything," said Odelia.

Dad frowned. "So who's the patient? You or Vesta?"

"Odelia," said Gran.

"Gran," said Odelia. She took a deep breath, then placed the pillbox on Dad's desk. "Gran has been taking these. She bought them off a drug dealer and thought they were vitamins, but in actual fact they're called ecstasy pills. They're—"

But Dad whistled through his teeth. "That wasn't very smart of you, Vesta."

"Oh, don't give me that sanctimonious crap," Gran said. "Just take my temperature or my blood pressure or whatever you quacks do to sick people around this place."

"You know perfectly well what we do to sick people around this place, Vesta," said Dad in his kindliest, most reasonable voice.

"Well, get on with it," she said. "Give me another lecture. God knows I've had to endure one lecture after another from my own granddaughter already."

"I'm not going to lecture you, Vesta," said Dad. "What I am going to do is tell you that these pills are the equivalent of a severe chemical shock to your system. A shock that at your age could very well have fatal consequences."

"Yeah, yeah, yeah."

Dad couldn't control himself any longer. "What the hell were you thinking?!"

"I was thinking they were vitamins! Vitamins!"

Dad listened to Vesta's heart, checked her pulse, listened

to her lungs, and did everything a doctor would after hearing that his septuagenarian patient has been popping ecstasy as if they were M&Ms. In the end, he pursed his lips.

"Just give it to me straight, Doc," said Vesta, looking up at her son-in-law with a modicum of trepidation written all over her features. "How long have I got?"

"You're actually in excellent fettle for a woman your age."

"My age!" she said, trepidation quickly giving way to indignation. "I'm a young woman!"

"Not that young," he said diplomatically. "As I said, for a woman your age you're in excellent health, and the pills don't seem to have done any damage to your system. I would like to take some blood, though, and have it examined."

She stuck out her arm resignedly. "Here. Take my blood, Count Dracula."

"So I'll see you tomorrow morning, completely sober."

"I never drink and you know it."

He smiled indulgently. "You know the drill, Vesta. First thing tomorrow morning I'm going to draw some blood and we're going to send it to the lab and then we'll know more."

She rolled her eyes. "Yeah, yeah, yeah. So are we done?"

"For now, we're done."

"Good. Let's get out of here, Odelia. This place makes me sick." And as they walked out, she muttered, "Too many sick people," and gave a cursory nod to Mrs. Baumgartner.

It was amazing, Odelia thought, that her grandmother, in spite of her age, and in spite of her shenanigans, was in such good health. Probably her character. God didn't want to snatch her up from this life and foist her on the next, so he'd decided to leave her be.

"Doctors," said Gran as she yanked down her seatbelt. "Always fussing, fussing, fussing. Why doesn't anyone ever believe me when I tell them I'm fit as a frolicking filly?"

"You keep falling asleep," Odelia reminded her.

"It's my naptime!"

She held up her hands. "Okay, okay. Fine."

"So what's next? Are we going to talk to this Animal person now?"

"I think I'm going to wait until Chase is free. He sounds like the kind of guy you don't want to meet without some muscle to back you up."

"I'll be your muscle," said Gran, stripping up her sleeve and flexing a non-existent bicep.

Odelia laughed. Looked like Gran was back to her old self, and she was glad for it. The woman might be a pain in the patootie, but she loved her to death.

"I want to drive by Jeb's place again. Check that fence where our mystery witness says he saw Jeb kill Camilla. And then I want to have another chat with Helena and Fae. Give them an update on the investigation."

"Good. Let's get going. I don't have all day, you know."

And as Odelia put the car in gear, Gran promptly dozed off again.

CHAPTER 29

Odelia parked her car on the road's shoulder, and we all got out.

"So what are we doing here?" asked Dooley.

"She wants to take a closer look at the fence," I said. "Remember the witness who came forward and said he saw Jeb and Camilla arguing, and then he actually saw Jeb attack Camilla? Well, the only way he could have seen that was if he was standing out there, looking in through a hole in the fence."

Dooley's attention was momentarily snagged by a couple of birds tweeting and twittering up a storm in a nearby tree, and I rolled my eyes. And as Odelia checked the fence, I followed close behind. Gran, meanwhile, was still sleeping in the car, her mouth open, and snoring like a lumberjack cutting a particularly thick piece of log. Whatever was in those pills she took, instead of bucking her up, they'd put her to sleep!

"I don't see it," said Odelia as we snuck closer to the fence. "Oh, there it is. See? There's a hole."

Actually, I couldn't see, for I'm a lot shorter and closer to the ground than she is. When I reminded her of this fact, she apologized and picked me up. And then I saw it, too. There was a hole in the fence that offered a perfect view of Jeb's so-called private lodge. From that particular vantage point, anyone could have looked in.

"So this witness was right," said Odelia. "Too bad he chose to remain anonymous."

"If he was walking his dog, it must be someone who lives around here," I said.

"Good point, and I'm sure Uncle Alec and Chase thought of that, too."

I suddenly noticed something odd. "That hole looks so nice and round. Is that normal?"

We moved closer, Odelia and me both studying the hole in more detail.

The fence was a chain-link contraption, covered with a sheet of dark green plastic to shield the area off from unwanted lookie-loos. But in the exact spot where Jeb's living room was, someone had cut a round hole of about a foot diameter.

Odelia crouched down and checked the ground, putting me down as well. There were green plastic shavings right below the hole. She checked them.

"These look pretty recent," she said.

"So what does that mean?"

She got up. "It means that someone wanted to spy on Jeb Pott. And that someone knew exactly where Jeb was going to be."

"Could be a reporter," I suggested. "Or a paparazzo."

"Could be," she agreed. "Or it could be someone who wanted to keep an eye on Jeb for a different reason."

"Like our Mr. Animal. The one Jeb owed money to?"

"You're right. Loan sharks want to keep an eye on their victims. Just in case they decide to make a run for it without paying. This Animal could have sent one of his goons out here to keep an eye on Jeb. And cut a neat hole in the fence just for that purpose."

It sounded reasonable, but still didn't explain... "Could it be that this goon was the one who called in the attack? It would stand to reason he wouldn't want his identity revealed to the police. Not if he was spying on Jeb."

"Do loan sharks care if their clients murder people?" asked Odelia, more to herself than to me.

"I would think so. A client in jail is a client who can't pay what he owes, and he can't be reached to put the squeeze on either. So it would be in the loan shark's best interest to prevent his client from going to prison."

"Loan sharks are usually part of a criminal organization. Their reach extends inside most prisons, so I don't think that would matter a great deal. No, this would have to be a loan shark with a conscience, which seems at odds with the profession."

"And the name. Animal," I reminded her.

She suddenly glanced across the street. "I like this idea of a neighbor a lot more, actually. Someone walking their dog. Which would put him in any of these houses. Lots of people don't want to get involved with the police, or see their names printed in the newspapers. People like their privacy, and coming forward as a witness carries a certain risk. Testimony in court, maybe, scrutiny from the press, potential backlash at work, etcetera. I would understand why this person would choose to remain anonymous. What bugs me is the burner phone. Why would a person walking their dog carry a burner phone? That doesn't fit with the idea that this is an ordinary neighbor, concerned about Camilla."

She was following a certain train of thought, I could tell, and suddenly turned and crossed the street, walking straight up the house located there. I followed her, hissing, "Dooley. Leave those birds alone!"

"Huh?" said Dooley, clearly in the throes of the bird spectacle.

For some reason birds flitting about in trees exact a powerful fascination on us cats. We can stare at them for hours upon hours. But now was not the time to practice ornithology. Now was the time to assist Odelia, who was clearly onto something.

"What about Gran?" asked Dooley, hurrying after us.

"Oh, she's fine," I said. "Sleeping off her ecstasy bender."

Odelia glanced through the windows of the house across the street. This was a more modest structure, compared to the place where Helena and her daughter lived. It was built flush with the road, without a front yard, and barely big enough to house a family.

"What are you thinking?" I asked.

"I'm thinking that if someone wanted to keep an eye on Jeb, this house would be the perfect place to do it from. As a matter of fact, this window is perfectly lined up with Jeb's window, visible through that hole in the fence."

"Careful," I said, "If this Animal is in there, he might not appreciate the company."

"Maybe we can take a quick peek inside," Dooley offered. "People are less intimidated by cats than by other people."

"Okay," Odelia said reluctantly. I could tell she was raring to barge into the house, to discover if her latest theory had any merit.

Dooley and I headed around the back, hoping to find some access point that would lead us into the house.

The house was clearly deserted, or had been allowed to dilapidate. The backyard was a tangle of weeds, and creepers covered the entire backside, the brickwork crumbling in places. I could see a hole in the roof, and several windows were broken.

We hopped inside through one of those broken windows on the ground floor, and discovered that the house was, indeed, derelict. No furniture, with mold covering the walls.

"Yuck," said Dooley. "What's that awful smell?"

"Rot," I said. "If you leave a place exposed to the elements like this, decay sets in, and before long nature takes over, reducing a sound structure to rubble within a few short years."

We tripped across the floor and searched around until we found the room Odelia had indicated.

"This is more than just decay, Max," said Dooley when we arrived in the room, which did, indeed, provide a perfect vantage point to watch the house across the street. A camera tripod stood lined up, but there was no camera mounted on top. Several cigarette butts littered the floor, as did fast-food wrappers, and an old couch had clearly been sat in.

"Someone's been here," I said.

"Odelia was right," said Dooley.

"So where is this person?" I asked.

I now became aware of the fact that Dooley had been right about the smell. This was not ordinary rot. This smelled more... coppery. Almost like... blood.

I stuck my nose in the air and sniffed, then let my keen sense of smell carry me to the source of the strange odor. In the hallway I found a door that led into the basement, the door itself dangling from its hinges. And as I stared down, my eyes quickly adjusting to the darkness, I noticed how several stairs were broken. And when I looked beyond them, I saw a large object lying on the cement floor below. It was a human being, and he wasn't moving...

CHAPTER 30

When Max and Dooley came racing out of the house, meowing up a storm, Odelia knew something bad had happened. Still she had the presence of mind not to go inside but instead to call her uncle. Within minutes, he arrived, Chase riding shotgun, and both men jumped out.

"There's a body of a man inside," she said, as she pointed to the house. "I mean," she quickly corrected herself, "I think there is. I'm not sure. You better take a look."

Chase checked through the window. "I don't see a thing."

"I have a hunch," said Odelia.

"Odelia has good eyes," said Uncle Alec. "Cat's eyes."

"Let's take a look inside," said Chase, then noticed how Gran was sitting in Odelia's car, her mouth open, still snoring up a storm. "Is she all right?" he asked, concerned.

"Don't mind her," said Alec. "She's taken ecstasy pills and is sleeping them off."

"Ecstasy," Chase repeated.

He had that Alice in Wonderland look on his face again, a

look he'd worn many times since making Odelia's acquaintance.

"Don't ask," said Alec. "So let's see who the dead guy is, shall we?"

They moved to the front door and it easily gave way, the wood having rotted away. Odelia followed in their wake, Max and Dooley keeping their distance. They didn't like the smell of dead people. Neither did she, but she needed to take a look anyway. This was her investigation, and the plot had just thickened considerably.

"Huh," said Chase as he let the light from his smartphone flicker over the man lying at the bottom of the basement stairs. The man had his eyes open, staring unblinkingly into space. "He looks pretty dead, all right." He turned to Odelia. "Are you sure you didn't go in?"

"I… I guess I must have smelled him," she said lamely.

She studied the man, then gasped. "I think I've seen him before."

"Who is he?" asked Uncle Alec.

"He looks like Jack Palmer. A reporter for the *Happy Bays Gazette*."

"The *Happy Bays Gazette*?" asked Alec. "What the hell was he doing here, then?" He took out his phone and called in an ambulance, as well as the county coroner's people.

Odelia and Chase moved to the living room, and studied the tripod. If a camera had been placed on top of it, it would have offered a perfect look into Jeb Pott's lodge.

"Looks like he was snapping pictures of Jeb," said Chase, checking the angle.

"He probably cut the hole," said Odelia. "Jack specialized in digging up dirt on celebrities. He must have heard Jeb was in town and decided to poke around."

"Looks like he found more dirt than he bargained for," said Chase.

"So if he was taking pictures of Jeb," said Alec, putting his phone away, "where is his camera?"

"Good question," Odelia murmured. There was no trace of a camera anywhere, or a phone, or a laptop.

"So let me get this straight. Our guy here comes into town to spy on Jeb. He stumbles down the stairs, breaks his neck, and his camera magically vanishes into thin air."

"He could have hidden it somewhere," said Odelia. "This place was crawling with reporters two days ago. If he took pictures of…" Her eyes widened. "What if Jack is our mystery caller—the anonymous witness?! If he was taking pictures of the house across the street, he could have seen the murder—he could have gotten the whole thing on film!"

"We need that camera," Alec muttered. "And by God I'm gonna find it, if I have to tear down this place to do it. If what you're saying is true, and I think it is, this cinches it."

Sirens could be heard in the distance, and Alec went outside to meet his people. Odelia found herself staring across the street, straight into Jeb's secret hideaway. Only his hideaway hadn't been as secret or hidden away as he would have hoped.

"What do you think?" asked Chase.

"Honestly? If Jack was the witness, that's it for Jeb. Game over." Then again, until they found that camera, all bets were off. She told him about their run-in with Conrad, and about Animal, the guy Jeb owed money to. She also touched on her conversations with Prunella Lemon and Fitz Priestley, and how little they'd yielded in fresh information.

"This Animal sounds like a good lead," Chase said. "Though I hope you're not thinking about approaching him all by your lonesome. Or, even worse, with your granny in tow."

"I was hoping you'd join me. I'd feel a lot safer with you backing me up than Gran."

"Although you have to admit your grandmother is a force to be reckoned with."

They both watched through the window as Gran woke up, stretched, then looked around, confused why she was alone.

"Odelia!" she yelled. "Where the hell are you? *Odeliaiaaaah!*"

Chase grinned. "Time to go back to grannysitting, babe."

Odelia rolled her eyes. "How are the kittens, by the way?"

"They've quickly turned into the talk of the station. Everyone—and I do mean everyone—has been finding excuses to go over and play with them. They're incredible."

"They are, aren't they?"

"Alec is even thinking about adopting them, so he can bring them to work. Turn them into the station mascots."

She laughed. "You're kidding."

"No, I'm not. He's crazy about those little guys, and so am I, by the way."

She placed an affectionate hand on his chest. "Crazy cat dude."

"You know it."

"Odeliaaaah!" Gran screamed. *"Odeliaaaaaaaah!"*

CHAPTER 31

For some reason I found mystifying, Gran was screaming for Odelia. Dooley and I walked up to her and told her Odelia was inside, and that we'd found a dead body.

"Not another dead body," said Gran, then suddenly seemed to get an idea. She grabbed her smartphone, got out of the car with surprising alacrity, and raced to the house.

"Where is she going?" asked Dooley.

"No idea."

"Don't move that body until I get there!" she was yelling. "Don't you dare move that body, Alec!"

She disappeared inside the house.

I shared a look with Dooley that spoke volumes. Humans, said that look. I know, Dooley's look returned.

We casually strode up to the house and jumped up on the windowsill, from where we had a perfect view of the happenings inside. Chase stood chatting with Odelia, Uncle Alec stood barking at one of his deputies, and Gran? She demanded to see the dead body.

"Weird," said Dooley.

"Really weird," I agreed.

"Bloodthirsty," Dooley added.

"Probably something to do with her vlog."

"Her vlog?"

"Video blog. Grandma has a video blog where she chronicles her sleuthing adventures. She probably figured it needed a bit more verisimilitude."

Dooley stared at me.

"Reality. She probably wants to add reality to her videos. Humans like blood."

"They do, don't they? I don't."

"Me neither." I couldn't even stand the sight of blood. Then again, we're cats, and therefore peaceable creatures. Except Clarice, maybe, with her strange taste for rats.

"So now what?" said Dooley.

"Now we have a bad-boy actor in jail for murdering his ex-wife, his daughter who believes he's innocent, a neighbor director who may or may not have harbored a grudge against Jeb for destroying his directing career, a bestselling novelist who may or may not have harbored a similar grudge against Jeb for destroying her noveling career, a dead paparazzo who was spying on Jeb and who may or may not have witnessed Jeb murdering his ex-wife and obtained photographic evidence, and a drug dealer and a loan shark who may or may not have wanted to get back at Jeb for not paying the money he owed."

"A right royal mess," was Dooley's opinion, and I was inclined to agree with him. "So who did it?"

"You mean, if we agree that Jeb didn't do it?"

"That's what we believe, right?"

"That's what his daughter believes. It's not necessarily what we believe."

"Oh, boy," he said. "This case is giving me a headache."

Odelia came walking out of the house, along with Gran,

and gave us a 'join me' sign.

"Where are we going?" I asked as we crossed the street again.

"I'm going to offer my findings to my client," she said.

We both looked puzzled, I guess, for Gran growled, "She's going to talk to that Fae Pott again, and tell her what we've discovered so far. It's what private investigators do. They keep their clients up to date."

"Oh, right," I said. "So did you get your pictures of the dead person, Gran?"

She directed a foul look over her shoulder. "Alec won't let me, the jerk. Calls it interfering with his crime scene. I asked him if he wanted my fist to interfere with his face and he said he was putting his foot down. And then when I put my foot down on his foot, he kicked me out of the house. He kicked out his own mother! Can you believe that?"

I could, and I did, and I silently commended Uncle Alec on showing backbone.

Odelia pressed the bell, and moments later the gate swung open and we were walking down the driveway in the direction of the house. Even before we arrived there, Fae and Helena were already coming out of the house to meet us.

"And? What have you found?" asked Helena.

"And what are all those policemen doing across the street?" asked Fae.

"They found a dead body," said Odelia.

"A dead body!" cried Helena. "Oh, dear lord."

She darted a quick look at her daughter and burst into tears, Fae patting her on the back. "It's going to be all right, Mom," said the girl. "Isn't that right, Odelia?"

Odelia nodded noncommittally, and we all moved inside.

I thought Helena looked even worse than the last time I'd seen her. Her eyes were red and puffy, and she was as pale as a ghost.

"She still loves Jeb," said Dooley, who'd also noticed the woman's distress.

"Yeah, she must have never stopped loving him," I said, "in spite of the fact that he left her for a younger woman."

Fae and Helena looked surprised that two cats followed in Odelia's footsteps.

"Odelia loves her cats," Gran explained. "They're like her good-luck charms."

"They are," Odelia confirmed. "I don't go anywhere without them."

"I adore cats," said Fae, kneeling down next to us and tickling our chins.

"I like her so much," said Dooley.

"You like every human who tickles you," I said. Well, so did I, actually. Fae certainly seemed nice. And I admired the way she stood up for her father and believed in his innocence, in spite of all the evidence against him. Loyalty like that was a rare trait.

As Odelia and Gran moved into the living room to give Helena and Fae an update on the investigation, Dooley and I took this opportunity to freely roam the house.

"Where is Sasha?" I asked, and just as I said it, the Bichon Frisé came tripping in from the kitchen, and greeted us like long lost friends.

"Max! Dooley! So nice to see you again!"

"Hey, Sasha," I said.

"Why don't I give you the grand tour this time?" the fluffy little doggie offered.

"That would be great!" I said, though I could have done without the escort. It's hard to snoop freely if the owner's lapdog is looking over your shoulder the whole time.

As it turned out, there wasn't all that much to be gleaned. In the study a large portrait of Jeb Pott was hung over the fireplace. It depicted him in his fresh-faced heyday, before he had allowed himself to become a little seedy around the edges. There were also a bunch of movie posters from the same period, and a stack of DVDs, ordered chronologically.

"Clearly his family never stopped loving him," said Dooley.

"Oh, no," said Sasha. "Helena is still devoted to Jeb. Loves him to death."

I shivered. I'd never cared for that particular expression.

We trudged up the stairs, to visit the master bedroom, which told us that Helena hadn't remarried, for we could detect only her smell there, and only one pillow on the bed.

The next bedroom belonged to the girl, Fae. More posters of Jeb on the walls, and even a doll depicting him as Captain Blood, his breakout role. A book was lying on the nightstand. It was called *When You Left Me*, and I scanned the blurb, more out of boredom than because I thought it would offer up any valuable clues.

"This is where I sleep," said Sasha proudly, jumping on top of the bed.

"Nice," I said, not all that interested. "Dooley and I sleep at the foot of the bed, too. Isn't that right, Dooley?"

"We sleep until our humans sleeps, then we hit the road," said Dooley.

"Yeah, we like to head out at night," I said. "Places to go, cats to see..."

"Harsh," said Sasha reproachfully. "I keep my human company all night long. I never leave her side—which is a lot of work," she added defensively when we merely stared at her. "I have two humans, you see, and I try to divide my time equally between them. Fair is fair. So if I've spent the morning with Fae, I try to spend the afternoon with Helena. And when I've spent one night with Helena, I try to spend the next night with Fae. Hard to keep up."

Looked like this dog needed a time management app.

"Look at this," said Dooley suddenly. I jumped down from the nightstand and joined him in front of what looked like a shrine dedicated to Fae's father's career. It was a photo display board, a linear depiction of his career, with snapshots from all of his movies and his life. There were also pictures of Jeb and his first wife together on holiday, pictures of Fae seated on Jeb's shoulder grinning at the camera in front of a snowy mountain peak. Fae and her daddy in Disneyland, riding one of the big rollercoasters and yelling at the camera…

"Poor girl," said Dooley.

"Yeah, it's sad," Sasha agreed.

"To have to watch your dad go to prison must be tough," I said. "I can totally see why she hired Odelia."

"I hope she proves Jeb's innocence," said Sasha.

"Fae could be wrong, of course. It's probably hard for a daughter to accept that her father is a ruthless killer."

"I hope she's right," said Sasha.

The three of us stared up at those pictures, and all heaved deep sighs.

Tough case.

"Max! Dooley!" Odelia's voice sounded from downstairs.

"That's our cue," I told Sasha. "Time to go."

"Oh, you can't leave yet," said the dog. "I haven't shown you my basket."

"Um… maybe next time," I said, really not all that interested in Sasha's basket. Now if she'd said she wanted us to see her food bowl…

We arrived in the foyer just in time to watch Odelia and Gran say their goodbyes to Helena and Fae. Helena had been crying again, and as we walked out she had trouble staying composed. We waved at Sasha, whom Fae had picked up, and the door closed.

CHAPTER 32

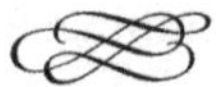

That night, two hooded figures could be seen walking the streets of some of the more shady nooks of Hampton Cove.

"Are you sure you want to do this?" asked one hooded figure.

"Not entirely," said the other.

They were none other than Odelia and Chase, who were determined to get in touch with a man who called himself the Animal.

Gran had wanted to tag along, too, but Odelia had strictly forbidden her. Meeting an animal like Animal was not suitable for old ladies, she'd said, to which Gran had responded with a particular gesture of the hand that was strictly R-rated.

"Are you sure we're going to find this guy there?" asked Odelia.

"Pretty sure. At least that's what my informant told me."

"Who is your informant?"

"You have your secrets, I have mine, babe," said Chase with a grin.

"You're not still sore about me refusing to reveal my sources, are you?"

"Of course not. Intrepid reporters have to protect their sources from savage cops like me."

"Ha ha."

Odelia's sources were Max and Dooley—not something she could reveal to Chase.

"So have you found out what happened to Jack Palmer yet?"

"Looks like he fell through the staircase and broke his neck. The place is pretty ramshackle."

"What about the missing camera?"

"We're still looking into that. I talked to his editor. He said he sent him down here to get the scoop on Jeb's life in the Hamptons and that's what he was doing at the house."

"No sign of a struggle, fingerprints, footprints…"

"Funny that you should ask. There are faint traces of brush strokes in both the living room, hallway, and in front of the entrance to the basement."

"As if someone was there, and tried to cover their tracks."

"Exactly. But so far that's all we've got. I'm still going over Jack's phone records, bank statements, anything that might shed some light on those final couple of days."

They'd arrived at a night club, pulsating music spilling out into the street, people standing around, smoking and drinking and laughing. It was called the Cocky Cauldron, and was one of the more popular clubs in Hampton Cove right now.

"Is he in there, you think?"

"That's what my sources told me."

"Let's take a look," she said, and took off her hooded sweater. Underneath, she was dressed in a sequined blue top, neon-pink leggings and glittery gold platform shoes. She was also wearing a blond wig.

Next it was Chase's turn. He took off his sweater and Odelia clapped a hand to her mouth to stop from bursting out laughing.

Chase did a little twirl. He was wearing a Superman cape, Superman shirt, and Superman leggings. "Ta-dah," he said. "How do I look?"

"Oh, I have to take a picture."

She took out her phone and made a selfie of the two of them. They looked priceless.

A burly bouncer opened the door, cocking an eyebrow at Chase, and they went in. A roaring wave of disco music greeted them, and the noise of hundreds of party people.

"How weird for a loan shark to own a gay disco!" Odelia shouted over the din.

"I really hope my informant is right about this—or else I'm about to make a gigantic fool of myself!" Chase shouted back.

Men dressed like bikers or cops or outfitted in black leather from head to toe stared at Odelia. She was probably the only woman in the club. But when they realized she'd dressed up as Agnetha Fältskog of ABBA fame, they greeted her with cheers and high-fives.

They reached the bar and Chase leaned over. "We're looking for Tino!" he shouted.

The bartender, who was dressed in a tank top and studded jockstrap, gestured to the far corner of the dance floor. Chase nodded his thanks and gave the guy his order. Loaded up with two daiquiris, they proceeded along the dance floor, threading their way through the dancing frenzy and slowly but gradually bearing down on their intended target: the Animal.

The music was pumping, and the crowd was wild, as a DJ spurred them on. Couples stood kissing and Odelia couldn't stop grinning as she followed Chase, who was like an icebreaker driving a wedge through the sea of gyrating and sweating bodies. His Superman outfit attracted a lot of attention, as did his fit physique, and several men seemed more than eager to have him fill their dance card. He stoically parried all attempts to be distracted from his mission, though, and, like a regular Superman, proceeded with laser focus.

Finally, they arrived at a booth on the other side, where a diminutive man who was dressed like Kermit the Frog sat with three burly bodyguards, overseeing the seething masses. One of the bodyguards was a man with a scar along his face, and the tattoo of a scorpion on his neck. Cicero. He did not look pleased to see either Chase or Odelia.

"Tino Krawczalis?" Chase asked, bending over to make himself heard.

Immediately, the bodyguards stirred, but Tino motioned for them to back off.

"Who wants to know?" he asked, blatantly checking Chase out.

"My name is Chase Kingsley, and this is Odelia Poole. Jeb Pott's daughter asked us to investigate his ex-wife's murder."

The guy gave Chase a long look of appraisal, then nodded to his beefy sidekicks, who made themselves scarce. Cicero, as he walked off, gave Odelia a lascivious glance, and when he grinned, showcased more metal in his mouth than a steelworks. She blithely ignored him.

Instead of inviting Odelia and Chase to join him in his booth, Tino got up and gestured for them to follow him. He weaved his way along the other tables, then placed his palm against a mirror. Something flashed green, and the mirror swung open. A hidden door.

On the other side was a room decorated like a small salon, all red velvet and gilt furniture. Privacy was absolute, and yet they could still see what was happening on the dance floor through a one-way mirror.

So this was how the owner of the infamous Cocky Cauldron got his kicks, Odelia thought.

Tino's nickname suited him: the man did look like an animal, though not the animal she'd anticipated. He looked like a frog, with outsized, heavy-lidded eyes and a squashed-up face. His Kermit the Frog suit sat snugly around a five-foot lithe frame. The guy was short.

If this man was the head of a crime syndicate, he certainly didn't look it.

Tino sank down onto a Louis XIV couch, and invited them to join him.

For a moment, they sat watching the masses moving to the pulsating beats, which filtered into the room, then he smiled and said, "Detective Kingsley. What do you think of my very own police mirror?"

Chase looked surprised. "You know who I am?"

"Of course. And you, Odelia Poole, reporter and sometime sleuth. I've followed both your careers with interest. I never thought I'd see the day you showed up in my place of business dressed like Superman and Agnetha Fältskog, though."

Odelia took off the wig. "I hate this thing," she admitted. "I don't understand how people can wear wigs and not want to take them off all the time. They're so itchy!"

"I agree with you there, Miss Poole," said Tino. "Now, tell me all about this Jeb Pott business. As you will readily understand, I have a keen interest in everything that has to do with that man."

CHAPTER 33

"It's come to our attention that Jeb owed you a great deal of money," said Chase, taking the lead.

"And you think I had something to do with the death of his ex-wife, implicating him in her murder as a way of putting the squeeze on him," said Tino.

"The thought had occurred to us, yes," Chase admitted.

Tino smiled a thin smile. "You know why I wear this uniform, Detective?"

"No, actually I don't."

"It doesn't exactly strike fear in the hearts of my enemies. I know that. But a frog has one advantage over your better-known predators: it lashes out and snaps up a bug in a fraction of a second. The bug never sees the end coming, and therefore has no defense. Creatures that look as benign and harmless as a common frog don't use fear to keep their enemies in line. They simply gobble them up when they're not looking."

"Do you gobble up your enemies when they're not looking?" asked Odelia.

"It's just a figure of speech, Miss Poole." He pointed at her.

"I read your pieces. They're well-written and entertaining. You're a skilled writer and I admire that. Detective Kingsley's talents lie elsewhere, and I'd be lying if I said I admired him as much as I do you."

"Okay, let's cut to the chase here, Tino," said Chase. "Did you have something to do with the murder of Camilla Kirby or not?"

"I could play games with you all night, Detective," said the club owner, pursing his lips and now looking completely like an actual frog. "But this is a matter that I want to see resolved as quickly as you. Jeb owes me money, that is correct. I loaned it to him out of the goodness of my heart, and because I'm a great fan of his work. Every day he spends locked up is a day he can't earn the money to pay me back. So why would I want to put him there?"

"You could have murdered Camilla to show Jeb you mean business."

"That's not how I operate. I may talk a big game but I'm not a murderer. I don't go around killing people's loved ones to put pressure on them. That kind of behavior is bad for business, and ultimately attracts too much attention from the wrong crowd." He gestured to Chase. "You, Detective Kingsley. And your uncle, Miss Poole. Attention I don't want or need. No, I'm afraid I had nothing to do with Miss Kirby's death, and I'm as anxious as you are to find out what happened. Did Jeb kill her? That would be too bad, because I'll probably forfeit my money. Did someone else kill her in order to frame Jeb? Also not in my best interests. So I sincerely hope you find whoever is responsible so that Jeb Pott can go back to making blockbuster movies, entertaining the masses and paying me back what he owes me."

He appeared to be telling the truth, Odelia thought. Though with a gangster you just never knew, of course.

"Maybe you can ask around," said Chase. "Maybe one of your associates knows something or heard something."

"I have asked around, as you can imagine, which is how I knew before you showed up here in your Superman costume that you're in charge of this case. But so far I haven't been able to find out anything that can shed light on the matter. But you could, Miss Poole."

"I could what?" she asked.

"Solve this case. I've followed your exploits eagerly, and you seem to have a knack for solving tough riddles. I'm sure that if you put your mind to it, you'll solve this one, too."

"I don't know. This is a particularly tough one."

"I know. It has stumped me, too." He blinked as he surveyed the scene beyond his private room. "Just look out there."

Odelia looked out there, and so did Chase.

"What do you see?"

"Um, a lot of people having a good time?"

"No, a lot of people *wanting* to have a good time, and hoping they'll find it. But in order to have a good time, you need to look beyond the obvious. Get in touch with your soul. Look for the truth within."

It all sounded a little new-agey for Odelia's taste, but she nodded anyway.

"What are you saying, Tino?" asked Chase.

"I'm saying that if Miss Poole wants to solve this murder, she needs to move beyond the obvious. To look inside—into her own heart. That's where she'll find all the answers."

Chase rolled his eyes, but Odelia thought he had a point.

"I think I see what you mean," she said.

"Right? I don't know why I just said that." He spread his arms. "A gift I got from my mother. She was a fortune teller, and had the gift of sight. She always said I had the same gift, but the only good it does me is when I read the people I do business with. And even then I get it wrong sometimes. Like with Jeb Pott. I thought he was a safe bet, and now it looks like he wasn't. So prove me right, Miss Poole. Prove to me that Jeb is not a killer, and that I was right about him all along."

As they walked home, Odelia pondered these words. "Look for the truth within," she murmured.

"Oh, don't you start believing that crap, too," said Chase. "He was just messing with you."

"I don't think so," said Odelia. "I think he really meant what he said, about having the gift and inheriting it from his mother."

"Tino Krawczalis's mother was a prostitute, and if she was a fortune teller she never advertised it."

"Still, she might have had the gift of sight."

So she needed to look inside to solve this particular murder. Only problem was, as much as she wanted to believe Tino, she had a hard time making sense of the mystery that surrounded the death of Camilla Kirby.

"I know what we have to do," she said, patting Chase on the arm.

"Don't tell me. You want me to look inside, too."

"I'm going to take out my whiteboard. And I'm going to do it right now."

"It's after midnight! I think you need to go to bed. Get some sleep. Look at this whole thing again with fresh eyes in the morning."

"Oh, we will go to bed, but first we're going to create an investigation board."

CHAPTER 34

"So who are our suspects?" asked Odelia.

Dooley and I and Harriet and Brutus were all seated in the front row, Odelia's captive audience. Bim, Bam and Bom were also there, although they were a lot less captive. In fact they downright ignored her, chasing each other's tails and gamboling about the room like a fluff-ball stampede.

On the couch sat Gran, looking sleepy, as well as Chase, Tex, Marge and Uncle Alec.

"Um…" said Marge. "Suspect number one is Jeb Pott, obviously? Even though I don't think he actually did it."

"Why not?" asked Tex. "He's the one with the blood on his hands."

"And the one who's in the pictures this Jack Palmer took," said Chase.

"What pictures?" asked Alec. "We still haven't found his damn camera."

"Jeb is such a sweetheart," said Marge. "I'm sure he's innocent. Remember that movie where he took such good care of his dear old mother? A man like that can never raise his hand in anger at anyone, not even a horrible person like Camilla Kirby."

"So you thought she was pretty horrible, too, huh?" said Gran.

"Oh, yes, for sure."

Odelia wrote at the top of her whiteboard the name Jeb Pott. In her effort to write as legible as she could, she stuck her tongue out, which I thought was pretty cute.

"Next," she said. "Who else could have done it?"

"Well, this man across the street," said Gran. "This reporter fella."

"Jack Palmer. But why would he kill Camilla?"

"Because... he disliked celebrities and wanted to teach Jeb a lesson?"

"Unlikely, but I'm still going to write it down," she said. Chase was rolling his eyes again.

"I saw that!" Gran said.

"You saw what?" asked Chase, feigning innocence.

"You were rolling your eyes at me!"

"It's called yoga for the eyes. It involves rolling the eyes and palming them and other things that are highly beneficial for your long-term eyesight."

"You are such a smart-ass. But you're a handsome smart-ass and I like you."

"Thank you, ma'am," he said with a grin.

"So we have Jeb and Jack Palmer," said Odelia, visibly proud of her work. "Next?" Instead of waiting for her audience to come up with more names, she decided to speed up the process and do it herself. After all, everyone was tired, and wanted to go to bed.

"Prunella Lemon, because Jeb ruined her career. Fitz Priestley, because Jeb ruined his career. Tino Krawczalis, because Jeb owed him money and he wanted to coerce Jeb to pay him. Conrad Jenkins—"

"Who's Conrad Jenkins?" asked Marge, who'd missed big chunks of the investigation on account of the fact that she'd been busy prepping monthly book club night at the library.

"He's Mom's drug dealer," Uncle Alec said.

"Vitamins!" Gran cried. "They were vitamins!"

"Oh, right," said Marge, nodding. "The vitamin dealer."

"How are you feeling now, Vesta?" asked Tex.

"I'll feel better if you tell me I don't have to give blood in the morning," she snapped.

"Looks to me like she's fine," said Alec, and Tex nodded emphatically.

"So who else is there?" asked Odelia, studying her board.

"There's Helena Grace," I said.

"Helena Grace?" Odelia didn't seem convinced. "Why would she want to kill Camilla?"

"Because she stole her husband?"

Odelia nodded slowly. "Uh-huh. Okay. And she would implicate Jeb, why?"

"Because Jeb left her and she wanted to get even."

"He's got a point, Odelia," said Gran.

Chase, who had only heard meowing, frowned. "Who's got a point?"

"Odelia," Gran was quick to say.

"What point? I'm not following."

"That's because you're not taking your vitamins," said Gran, patting the cop's arm.

"I said that Helena is also a suspect," said Odelia, jotting down the woman's name.

"I must have missed that part," said Chase, and rubbed his eyes.

"And you can add Fae, too," I said. "After all, she might have held a grudge against her father's new wife, too."

"Fae Pott," said Odelia, and wrote down the name.

"Why Fae?" asked Chase.

"Because she was harboring a grudge against Camilla," said Odelia, repeating my words.

"Right," said Chase. "Unlikely, though. The girl is clearly crazy about her dad. And she hired you to investigate the murder. Would she do that if she was guilty?"

"Unlikely," Odelia agreed, and put Fae's name between brackets, and then Helena's name as well. "Helena is clearly very sad that Jeb is in jail," she explained. "And that kind of sadness can't be faked, no matter how great an actress she is."

"She does look very sad," Dooley agreed. "In fact she was crying even more the second time we saw her than the first."

"Can we speed this up?" asked Harriet. "I need my beauty sleep."

"I'm not following," said Brutus. "Are you following, Max?"

"So far, so good," I said, though I had to admit the case was pretty complicated.

"Okay," said Odelia. "Now for the other suspects. Conrad?"

"Has an alibi," said Uncle Alec, who sat slumped in his chair, clearly ready to nod off. "He was being 'entertained' by one of his customers at her place, and she swears up and down that he didn't leave the house at any point during the night."

"Tino Krawczalis?" asked Odelia, going over the list from bottom to top.

"Also has an alibi," said Uncle Alec. "He was in New York that night, opening a new club. Plenty of people saw him."

"Was he dressed in his Kermit costume?" asked Odelia with a giggle.

"He was," Alec confirmed. "He seems to like that particular outfit."

"Okay, moving on. Fitz Priestley."

"His wife says he was with her all night."

"Prunella Lemon. Husband provided her with an alibi."

"Not sure how strong those spousal alibis are, though," said Alec. "Wives and husbands tend to say anything to protect their partners, so I wouldn't take them off your list for now."

Odelia tapped the name at the top of the list. "That leaves us with Jeb Pott."

"Admit it, babe," said Chase. "He's still our number one suspect. He had means, motive, and opportunity, and from where I'm sitting he's guilty as hell."

"Tough for his ex-wife and kid," said Tex, rubbing his eyes.

Everyone looked tired, and it was time to go home.

"I think maybe I should tell Helena and Fae I have to disappoint them but that I haven't found conclusive evidence of anyone other than Jeb being behind the murder of his ex-wife," said Odelia. "And as soon as Jack's camera turns up, I'm afraid that's it for Jeb."

"So what about this Jack Palmer?" asked Gran. "Could he have done it?"

"I don't see why he'd kill a woman he's never even met," said Odelia.

"His death is definitely an accident, right?" asked Marge.

Odelia looked at her uncle, who nodded. "No sign of foul play. The guy stepped on a rotten step and broke his neck. Case closed."

And so was the meeting apparently, for everyone got up and started moving to their respective dwellings.

As far as I was concerned, it was obvious I didn't have anything useful to contribute to this particular case, so Dooley and I followed Odelia and Chase up to bed, and Harriet and Brutus followed Gran and the others to the house next door.

And as I settled in for the night, or at least until Odelia

was fast asleep, I said, "This is just about the weirdest case we've ever been involved in, don't you agree, Dooley?"

"Yeah, we caught the killer even before the investigation got started."

"Not every case has to be the same, though," I said, and placed my head on my paws.

And then I dozed off. It had been a long day, and since the case was apparently closed now, the culprit in jail, I decided not to spend another moment of my precious time on this investigation. What? I could have finished an entire bag of Cat Snax in that time.

CHAPTER 35

The next day, Marge decided to take her cat menagerie to work. Just as a special treat for us. Chase didn't mind taking the kittens to the police station again, but Marge felt that everyone deserved to have a chance to play with them, and there were so many kids who'd asked about the kittens when Marge had announced her daughter had recently adopted three of them, that she felt she really needed to show them off now.

So in the car we all went and onward to the library—no less than seven cats in the backseat, four of them adults and three babies.

Bim, Bam and Bom, of course, were playing around in the car footwell to their heart's content, the rest of us stodgy old cats perched neatly on our seats, not moving an inch.

"You know, Max?" said Brutus as he surveyed the tiny bundles of joy cavorting about, "when I see those kittens I suddenly feel old."

"Same thing here," I admitted. "For one thing, if I drop down from a great height I don't recuperate as well as those little tykes do."

"I don't see what the big appeal is," said Harriet, who still hadn't warmed to the youngsters.

"They're just so much fun to be around," said Dooley. "In fact they don't make me feel old—they make me feel young!"

"Oh, that's just crap," said Harriet. "You're only as old as you feel, and I, for one, refuse to believe in that age-old ageist nonsense. I feel young, therefore I am young."

"Yes, but they really are young," Brutus said, "whereas we are old—um, old-*er*," he quickly amended when she shot him a terse look.

Bom had discovered Harriet's fluffy tail again and now sat chewing on it. When she found out, she swiped at the young whippersnapper, but he didn't seem to mind. He probably thought it was a game, so he slapped her right back. After a while the other two kittens wanted in on the action, and they all started playing with Harriet, who kept trying to fend them off. The harder she tried, the more they crawled all over her.

"Oh, for Pete's sakes," she grumbled, and finally managed to swing one kitten in my lap, the second one in Dooley's and the third in Brutus's.

I grinned at the little one, and when she dug her tiny teeth into my tail, I didn't even mind. I'd grown to like the little angels—or devils, depending on how you felt about them.

We arrived at the library and Marge bundled up the kittens then let us walk into the side entrance under our own steam. We'd been there plenty of times before. The kids had so much fun playing with us that I always loved our time at the library. Even the old folks enjoyed our company. They always said being around us cats brought them so much joy that they returned home happy as clams. And so did we, actually.

"You know, Marge," I said as I accompanied her to the counter, where she booted up her computer. "I once heard about a nursing home where the staff keeps all kinds of pets. Piglets, chickens, puppies, cats—you name it. The pets just wander around, and it makes the old folks so happy, lowers their blood pressure, and creates a very pleasant atmosphere."

"That's exactly what I'm trying to accomplish here," she said. "Only I try to make it fun for everyone, not just the elderly."

"Like a petting zoo—but at the library. A library zoo."

She laughed. "Something like that."

I jumped up on her desk. "Do you really think the murder case is closed now?"

"I guess so," she said. "They caught Jeb, didn't they? Such a shame, though, right? I really liked him. Of course, you never know what people are really like. Some actors that you think are nice turn out to be horrible people in real life. I guess you just never know."

The kittens were having a great time over in the pirate ship, where Marge had dropped them, and were sinking their tiny claws into the pillows. The library opened in half an hour, and then the fun would begin. Dooley and Brutus and Harriet, meanwhile, had gone off to the kitchen, to see if Marge had filled up their bowls with the right amount of food and drink. There were also plenty of litter boxes and climbing poles and even toys.

As Marge sat typing something on her computer, I allowed my gaze to drift idly to the book cart loaded with plenty of tomes she still needed to put back on the shelves.

I was struck by the title of one of the books: *When You Left Me.*

"Hey, that's funny," I said. "That's the book Fae Pott is reading."

"Mh?" said Marge, without looking up.

"*When You Left Me.* Young adult, probably?"

"What?" said Marge, looking up and taking off her reading glasses.

I pointed to the book. "It was lying next to Fae's bed. I read the blurb. Something about a girl whose daddy starts a second family. Sounds like appropriate reading for Fae."

Marge took out the book, and I noticed how her hands were shaking.

"Oh, no," she whispered.

"Oh, yes," I assured her. "She must have read it a lot. It was well-thumbed."

She looked up at me, and I could tell she was distressed.

"I have to call Odelia at once," she said softly.

"Great," I said, for lack of anything better to say.

Humans. You think you finally got them figured out, and then you realize you've only skimmed the surface.

CHAPTER 36

Odelia listened carefully. She frowned as the realization hit her.

"Are you sure about this, Mom?"

"Of course I'm sure. Max told me so himself."

Odelia sank down on the couch. She'd been getting ready to go to work, but this changed everything. "It's hard to believe," she said.

"I know!"

"Look, I need to make a few phone calls. I'll call you back as soon as I know more."

"That's fine—do what you have to do, but honey?"

"Yes?"

"Please be careful, all right?"

"Of course. I'm perfectly safe here." Her mother disconnected and Odelia sat staring before her for a few beats. Then she took a deep breath and dialed her uncle's number.

"Odelia?" he said, picking up on the first ring.

"There's something I need you to check for me," she began.

"Sure. Anything."

In a few words, she told him what her mother had discovered.

He sounded as shocked as she was when Mom told her about the book.

"I'll get back to you," said Uncle Alec. "Have you told Chase yet?"

"Not yet. You know how he is about mystery witnesses and phantom sources."

"You can always tell him you saw the book but only realized its significance when you picked up a copy at the library."

It seemed like a good solution. "You better tell him," she said. "I'm such a terrible liar I'll probably make some mistake and then he'll become all suspicious again."

"And I'm a better liar than you, is that what you're saying?"

"You're a cop. You have to be the better liar."

"Fair point," he conceded, then hung up.

She waited with bated breath, thinking things through once more. The whiteboard still sat in the middle of her salon, right next to the television. She'd switched on the TV to watch the news, and now saw an item about Jeb Pott. She walked over and turned up the sound. Jeb was about to be arraigned and appear before a judge. Bail would probably be an exorbitant sum, that he almost certainly couldn't afford. He was going away for a long time.

She turned off the TV and stared at the whiteboard. Amazing. A long list of suspects, and the only person she'd never seriously considered even for a single second…

Her phone rang and she picked up. "Uncle Alec?"

"You were right. There were marks on his back. And we found the pictures."

"Then it's true," she said, and felt her heart constrict.

"Oh, yes, it's true. No doubt about it. The pictures tell the whole story."

"Oh, God," she said and felt tears spring to her eyes. She wiped them away.

"You did good, Odelia."

"My cats did good," she said.

"But it's you that figured it out."

Just then, her front doorbell rang. She said, "I have to go. Keep me informed."

"I'll let you know as soon as we've made the arrest."

She moved to the front door and opened it wide. She was surprised to find Fae Pott standing there, a charming smile on her youthful face.

"Hey, Odelia. I hope I'm not disturbing you?"

"No, not at all," she said. "Come on in."

The young woman darted into the house. "I was hoping you had some more news about my father's case," she explained, and stepped in front of the whiteboard. "Is this…"

"A list of suspects, yes," she said, as she joined Fae.

"Wow. I don't even know who most of these people are."

"It's not important. I think I've finally figured out what happened."

Fae turned to her, her expressive eyes wide. "You have?"

Odelia nodded. "I know who killed Camilla Kirby."

The two women shared a long look, with Fae searching Odelia's face for clues. "So?" she finally asked with a laugh, when she couldn't stand the tension anymore. "Who did it?"

She looked so young, Odelia thought. So young and innocent.

"It took me a while to put two and two together," she said, taking a seat on the couch. "I actually just got off the phone with my uncle. He's going to make the arrest now."

"But that's great! So it wasn't Daddy?"

"No, it wasn't your father."

Fae smiled a dazzling smile. "That's wonderful news!" She held out her hands. "Is it all right if I just wash my hands real quick? I came over on my bike, and my chain fell off."

"You can go upstairs. Bathroom is straight ahead."

The young woman bounded up the stairs like a filly. She was dressed in denim shorts, a white polo shirt and sneakers. As she mounted the stairs, Odelia found herself staring at those sneakers.

"So how did you find out?" asked the girl.

Odelia got up from the couch and moved to the foot of the stairs.

"Oh, just a coincidence, really," she said.

Water splashed in the bathroom. "Coincidence? What do you mean?"

She slowly took the stairs. "Remember yesterday? When I was at your house?"

"Of course."

"A friend of mine took the opportunity to look around."

"A friend? What friend?"

"That's not important. He searched your room, Fae."

"My room? Why?"

"Just being thorough. It's what good detectives do. Crossing T's and dotting I's."

"Oh, sure. That's how you get your guy, right? Leaving no stone unturned."

"He saw the book, Fae."

"What book?"

"*When You Left Me?*"

The water stopped running.

"You'll remember the book, you've read it more than once. It's about a girl whose CEO dad one day ups and leaves and decides to start a new family with his executive assistant. Her mother is so unhappy and depressed that the girl devises a diabolical plan. She decides to murder her father's new girlfriend, and do it in such a way that the blame falls squarely on him, thereby killing two birds with one stone: the girlfriend is dead, and the father will spend the rest of his life in jail, punished for a crime he didn't commit."

Silence.

"We also found your footprints on Jack Palmer's back, Fae. What happened? He saw how you killed Camilla and blackmailed you? So you shoved him down the stairs? You were lucky nobody saw you then."

"You're crazy," Fae said suddenly, materializing next to Odelia.

Odelia was startled, but only for a moment. "No sense denying, Fae."

The girl laughed. "All this from a book I read? A little far-fetched, Odelia."

"It's over," she said. "My uncle found Jack Palmer's pictures on his cloud computer. Oh, yes, reporters sync their work with the cloud. Just in case they lose their camera or it gets stolen—or is snatched like you did with Jack's camera after you killed him. We know you did it, Fae. We have the pictures and you're in them, murdering Camilla, then putting the knife in your father's bed and smearing her blood all over him."

Fae's face turned up into a wicked smile. "Pretty neat touch, huh? I actually used an eye dropper to sprinkle her blood all over my dad. Some of it even got into his ears. No way to deny his guilt, right? And then I called it in—lowering my voice and pretending to be a neighbor walking his dog. I watched from a distance when the cops came to arrest my dad. I jumped with joy as they led him outside and locked him up. Just what the bastard deserved for breaking Mom's heart," she added, her smile morphing into an expression of contempt.

"And what about Jack Palmer?"

She shrugged. "Like you said, he wanted money. A lot of money. So I killed him. Kicked him down the stairs. Too bad about those footprints, though. I was so careful not to leave any prints—didn't think about the footprints on his back," she said thoughtfully, staring down at her feet.

"Yeah, too bad about that," said Odelia softly. "How could you, Fae? How could you do that to your father? I thought you loved him?"

Her face turned bitter. "I loved him and I thought he loved me. Until one day he abandoned us for some stupid bimbo who made his life a living hell. So when he came crawling back to us, I decided my mother had been pushed around enough, and now it was his turn to experience some of the pain he'd caused. I just wish I'd killed him, too. I could have made it look like a murder-suicide but I figured that was too good for him."

"And what about Camilla? She didn't deserve to die."

"Oh, yes, she did. She broke up a good marriage, just so she could advance her career. She was the most horrible woman imaginable. And then when she finally got her big break she dumped my dad like yesterday's trash. What a bitch."

"I think you better come with me now. I'll take you to the police station."

"You should have seen the look on Camilla's face when I opened the door. And then when I stabbed her she was so shocked she actually started squealing like a pig!"

"Let's go," said Odelia, grabbing Fae's arm.

But the girl yanked herself free. She smiled sweetly. "I should never have hired you, should I? I thought I was being clever—no one would ever suspect me. Oh, that poor little girl whose daddy is in jail." The smile suddenly disappeared, and Fae's eyes turned vicious. "I always wanted to say this. Odelia Poole—you're fired!" And before she could stop her, she'd given Odelia a hard shove that propelled her backward down the stairs.

CHAPTER 37

For a moment she was flying through the air, and then she was tumbling, head over heels, the floor racing up to her before she smacked down on it with a painful thunk.

"That's what you get for messing with me!" Fae yelled from the top of the stairs.

Odelia, who'd miraculously landed without great injury, groaned, and said, "You'll never get away with this, Fae."

"Oh, yes, I will. I already told my mom what I did and she's taking us to a non-extradition country just in case." She stepped over Odelia, who grabbed her leg.

Fae tried to kick free, but Odelia held on, and managed to drag the young woman down. She was screaming and fighting like a wildcat, but Odelia was bigger and stronger, and pinned her to the ground.

"Get off me, you stupid jerk!"

"Not a chance," Odelia panted.

"Why couldn't you break your neck, like that stupid reporter!"

Suddenly, just when she thought she wouldn't be able to hold onto the squirming woman, the door suddenly flew open and her uncle burst through, followed by Chase and three more cops.

"How did you get here so quick?" asked Odelia, releasing Fae into Chase's hands.

"We went over to her place to make the arrest," said Alec. "Her mother told us she'd gone out. We figured she just might have come here to pay you a visit."

"You're hurt," said Chase, crouching down with a look of concern on his face.

"Just a scratch," she said, then, when she tried to get up, sank back down again. "Ouch."

"Serves you right!" yelled Fae, but Chase made short shrift of the young woman, and outfitted her with a pair of handcuffs, then handed her over to his colleagues, who read her her rights and escorted her outside.

"Looks like I may have twisted my ankle going down," said Odelia with a grimace.

"Oh, babe, why does this keep happening to you?"

"Because our Odelia is a born sleuth, that's why," said Uncle Alec. "I can't believe you cracked this case, honey."

"I had a stroke of luck," she said modestly.

"More like a stroke of genius," said Chase. He gently touched her ankle and she winced. "Let's take you to the hospital," he suggested.

"Oh, not again," she said. "I'll be fine. Just don't let Fae get away."

"She's not going anywhere," said Alec.

"She's a nasty piece of work. You know that she actually took great delight in killing Camilla? She was practically glowing when she told me what she'd done. Proud, you know."

“I could see it in the pictures,” said Alec. “There’s even a video. The woman is some kind of juvenile psychopath.”

“And to think I actually felt sorry for her. Actually thought she was pretty great.”

“She probably is, until you cross her. Then she turns vicious.”

The door swung open again, and Mom burst in, followed by Dad and Gran, and no less than seven cats.

Odelia laughed. The gang was all there.

Max hopped into her arms. “Are you all right?” he asked, his voice husky with worry.

“I’m fine, you guys. Just banged up a little bit.”

Dad knelt down next to her and did a cursory examination. “This is getting old,” he said sternly. “You need to take better care of yourself, young lady. I don’t want to have to keep finding you passed out on the floor of your own home.”

“Dad! You make it sound as if I’m some kind of lush!”

“You do need to be more careful, honey,” said her mother.

“I promise!”

For the sake of her newly arrived audience, she repeated, beat by beat, what had just transpired. They all followed the story with rapt attention, even the kittens.

And when she finished, Mom said, “I should never have called you about that book!”

Dad said, a catch in his voice, “You could have been killed!”

“But I wasn’t!” she said. “Relax, you guys. I’m fine.”

Finally, Gran said, “So there’s a video of this Fae girl killing Camilla?”

“Yes, there is,” said Uncle Alec, but then caught Gran’s intense look. “Oh, no. You’re not posting that horrible video on your YouTube channel!”

“Oh, yes, I am.”

"No, you're not! That's police evidence. Besides, that video is too graphic to post."

"I need this, Alec. Scarlett Canyon…"

"Not with that woman again!"

And as Alec and Gran took their discussion outside, the others all laughed heartily. Even Odelia laughed, even though her ankle hurt like hell, and other parts of her body that had come into contact with an unyielding staircase were now starting to hurt pretty badly, too.

And as Chase helped her up and moved her over to the couch, there was a knock on the door.

A woman stepped inside and glanced nervously at all the people present. She was pale and thin, her hair limp and lifeless, but her eyes shone with the fire of determination.

"Um... hi," she said. "Odelia Poole?"

"That's me," said Odelia.

"Hi, my name is Elsie Delaney. You don't know me, but... I know you—or know of you. From your articles in the Gazette? And um... I'm the one that left three kittens on your doorstep a couple of days ago. So…" She was wringing her hands now, and when she suddenly saw the threesome, who were dangling from the curtains again, she haltingly smiled, then released a stifled sob. "I'm so sorry, but... my husband left me last week and I guess I just… lost it. So I thought to give them to you, as you always write about cats with so much love, and…"

"Well, I've taken good care of them," said Odelia.

"Thank you so much," said Elsie with a watery smile. "And I'm so, so sorry. I should never—I realized the next day I'd made a big mistake. I love cats. And I should never have done this. It's just that... I was desperate. Desperate to move away from here—far away. I'm pretty sure my husband will get the house in the divorce, and I planned to move back in with my parents in Massachusetts. But then a friend convinced me yesterday to give Hampton Cove one more chance. She's going to help me find an apartment I can afford, and I realized that I… I have a job down at the senior center… and my colleagues are all so nice to me, and…" She suddenly broke down and started weeping, her shoulders shaking uncontrollably.

Odelia got up from the couch and limped over to the woman. She then held her in a warm hug. "I understand," she said softly. "Of course I understand. And it's fine."

And she did. And it was.

Odelia held her for a long time, until the sobs subsided. Marge handed her a tissue, and Elsie gratefully took it. "I'm so sorry," she said. "You must think I'm an idiot."

"We don't," Marge assured her. "We've all been there, sweetie."

Elsie glanced at the kittens, and Odelia could see the love in her eyes.

"You can have them back," she said. "Only I already named them. Bim, Bam and Bom."

Elsie laughed through her tears. "Bim, Bam and Bom?"

"My grandmother's idea. Admittedly, she's a little crazy."

Elsie laughed again, and then Odelia led her over to the curtains, where the three little babies were dangling happily. Odelia plucked them from her curtains and handed them to Elsie, who hugged them with such tenderness Odelia knew she was doing the right thing.

"Thanks," said Elsie with a shaky voice. "From the bottom of my heart, thank you."

"There's one condition, though."

"Anything."

"I can come visit them. And they can come visit us. Cause we've grown very fond of these three little babies."

"Of course," said Elsie. "As much as you want."

Suddenly a loud snuffle could be heard. They all looked down. It was Harriet.

"Are they going away?" asked the white cat.

Odelia nodded, and Max confirmed, "They're going back home."

"I'm going to miss them," said Harriet. "They're so cuuuuuuuuuuuute!"

EXCERPT FROM PURRFECTLY CLUELESS (THE MYSTERIES OF MAX 12)

Chapter One

I watched on with a modicum of weariness and exasperation as my human packed her weekend bag. Usually when Odelia goes on a trip she cordially invites me and Dooley along with her, and sometimes even Harriet and Brutus. Now, she was going away for the weekend and I wasn't invited!

Odelia was in no frame of mind to discuss what was obviously a grave oversight on her part. She was frowning so furiously I thought those grooves lining her brow would become permanently etched into her fair skin.

"Lemme see," she muttered. "Toiletries, check, phone charger, check, laptop and charger, check..." She heaved a deep sigh and her eyes flicked to her wardrobe. "Chase!" she suddenly cried. "Chase—where are you?!"

"What's wrong, babe?" Chase asked, as he came running.

She flapped her arms like a chicken. "I have nothing to wear!"

Chase heaved a sigh of relief. "I thought you were in trouble."

"I am in trouble! I'm going to spend the weekend with the most gorgeous, most successful, most iconic actresses of our time and I've got nothing to wear!"

Chase moved over to the closet and gave it a critical look. He let his hand trail along the outfits. "You've got plenty of stuff, honey. Any of these will do."

She gave him a scathing look, the kind that says: of course you would say a dumb thing like that. You're a guy!

"I need my mom," she said, and Chase left the room, realizing he didn't fit that particular description. Moments later, Odelia opened the bedroom window and hollered, "Mom! I need you in here! Now!"

It was a testament to her nervous condition that she would resort to shouting at her mother like that. Usually Odelia is the most mild-mannered human any cat could ever hope to be adopted by. Today she was giving every indication of being on the verge of a nervous breakdown.

Like Chase, I decided to return downstairs. Things were looking pretty grim, and I needed my best buddy to confide in and commiserate with.

Dooley watched me descend the stairs with a hopeful look on his face. But when he caught my expression that hope was quickly squashed like a bug.

"No dice?" he asked, just to be sure.

"No dice," I confirmed. "She's not taking us and that's her final word." And even if I wanted to try and convince her, I knew from long association with Odelia that now wasn't the time. "She's having trouble packing," I explained as I took position next to Dooley on the couch. "Doesn't know what to wear."

"Oh," he said, immediately understanding.

"Yeah."

"So that's that, then."

"That's that," I agreed.

We both stretched out on the couch and stared before us, musing about what could have been.

Marge came in through the sliding glass door and directed an anxious look at us. I said, "Nothing to wear," and Marge immediately understood, for she nodded once, plastered a look of determination on her face and proceeded up the stairs.

Odelia has always been a nervous packer, and now, with her star-studded weekend coming up, things were even worse than usual. For a reporter this is a highly unusual situation, you might say, but then Odelia is not one of your globe-trotting reporters who practically live in their suitcases. She doesn't traverse the Sahel in a beat-up Jeep with only a toothbrush and her wits. She doesn't look to interview rebels in the jungles of war-torn Angola. She's a small-time reporter for a small-town rag called the *Hampton Cove Gazette*, so she hardly does any traveling at all. This weekend was an exception, therefore, and I could see why this would exacerbate the situation to the point she needed her mother to help negotiate the packing of her weekender case.

Next to us, Chase had also taken a seat, and now the three of us were waiting, like expectant parents awaiting news from the maternity ward, or the Catholic flock in Saint Peter's Square for white smoke from the papal chimney.

"I still think she should have invited us," said Dooley.

"What's done is done, Dooley," I said, though I couldn't agree more.

"But why? Why doesn't she want to take us?"

"Because Emerald Rhone is allergic to cats."

Emerald Rhone, the most famous actress of our time, was allergic to cats. It was hard to believe and yet it was true. The moment I heard it, I experienced a slight diminution of my love and timeless admiration for the screen legend.

"I still find it hard to believe Odelia would be invited to

spend the weekend with Emerald Rhone," said Dooley. "Does she even know her?"

"I doubt it. As far as I know Odelia's boss wangled the invitation."

Dan Goory, editor of the *Hampton Cove Gazette* and Odelia's boss, prides himself on being the most well-connected man in the Hamptons. His address book is a veritable Who's Who of the rich and famous, and among those luminaries, apparently, is the one and only Emerald, the greatest living actress.

"I can't believe Emerald is allergic to cats," said Dooley.

"I can't believe it either and yet it is so," I said.

We both mused on this most unthinkable thing for a while.

"Now I don't even like her anymore," said Dooley finally. "And I wish I hadn't watched her lousy show."

The show he was referring to was *Big Little Secrets*, which had been a huge ratings hit and had apparently been watched by everyone and their cat. Now that the final episode had aired, the star cast of the show were meeting for the weekend at Emerald's Hamptons home, on the outskirts of Hampton Cove. All five stars were going to be there: Kimberlee Cruz, Verna Rectrix, Abbey Moret, Alina Isman and of course Emerald herself. And Odelia and Chase.

Normally Dan Goory would have gone, as an old friend of Emerald's, but since he had a prior engagement—he was doing a golf tournament in Scotland—he'd decided to send Odelia as his celebrity emissary instead.

Chase suddenly glanced over in our direction. I gulped a little. I know that Chase, Odelia's cop boyfriend, doesn't speak our language, but sometimes I wonder. The man is part of the family, after all, and you never know if Odelia's gift of talking to her cats can be transferred by close association.

"So what do you guys think?" asked Chase now.

"Think about what?" I asked cautiously.

"Is she going to come out of this thing with her sanity intact or should we call off the whole thing?"

"Oh, Marge will fix her right up," said Dooley. "She always does."

Chase gave us a bemused look and chuckled lightly. "You guys are so funny. Do you know that before I met you I never even considered cats as intelligent creatures? I always thought that honor was reserved for dogs."

Both me and Dooley bridled. "Dogs!" I said, stiffening. "Please don't compare us with that foul and horrid breed, Chase. I mean, please!"

"Yeah, dogs are no match for cats," Dooley added.

"No comparison," I agreed. "Like, at all."

Chase had narrowed his eyes at us. "Sometimes I wish I could understand what you're saying. It almost strikes me as meaningful." Then he shook his head. "What am I doing? Talking to a bunch of cats. I must be losing it."

He was losing it, if he was comparing us to dogs. But I decided not to press the point. Chase was obviously under a great deal of stress. He was, after all, Odelia's plus-one for this shindig, and probably just as nervous as she was.

Then again, he didn't look nervous. In fact he looked as cool as a cucumber. A little bored, even. As if he wasn't particularly looking forward to visiting acting royalty as much as Odelia was.

He finally heaved a deep sigh and checked his watch. "If she keeps this up we're going to be late."

Dooley eyed me meaningfully.

"No, Dooley," I said. "We're not going to ask Chase to take us along. For one thing, he doesn't understand what we're saying, and for another, he's a self-declared dog person, and everyone knows dog persons aren't exactly advocates for the rights of cats to join their humans wherever they go."

"Please, Max," he said. "The least we can do is try."

I rolled my eyes. "Oh, all right." So I tapped Chase lightly on the arm.

He looked up. "Mh?"

"Chase," I said, enunciating clearly and deliberately.

"What is it, buddy?" he said, frowning.

This was good news. Maybe he could understand me after all? "Could you please tell Odelia she needs to bring us along on this weekend trip?"

"Yes, please, Chase," said Dooley, giving the burly cop his best puss-in-boots look.

Chase eyed us both curiously for a moment, then laughed. "If I didn't know any better I'd say you guys want to tag along this weekend, don't you?"

"Oh, yes, please!" said Dooley eagerly.

He laughed again. "Fine," he said finally. "I'll take it up with Odelia." He then got up and started pacing the living room floor. "What's taking her so long? She could have packed for a year by now, let alone a weekend."

Dooley and I shared a happy look. Chase was taking up our case.

Which meant we were going on a little trip after all!

Chapter Two

Odelia had navigated the streets leading out of town deeply lost in thought. It was only when she passed the sign welcoming people to Hampton Cove, the friendliest place in the Hamptons, that she finally realized Chase was talking. She'd been driving on auto-pilot for the past couple of minutes and now looked up. "I'm sorry, what were you saying?"

"I think your cats wanted to tag along," he said, much to her surprise.

"My cats?" She cut him a quick sideways glance. "Did they... tell you that?"

It wasn't possible. Only the women in her family had the gift of being able to talk to cats. Not even her uncle Alec could understand them.

"Yeah, they were putting on a real show while you were upstairs with your mother. Meowing or mewling or mewing or whatever the hell it is that they do." He shook his head. "I gotta tell you, babe. Sometimes those cats of yours could almost pass for humans the way they go on. And the way they look at you! Staring with something akin to actual intelligence in those big eyes."

"Well, cats are highly sensitive and intelligent creatures."

"That, they are. Especially yours." He settled back, stretching out his long legs. "Now are you finally going to relax and enjoy this trip? Ever since Dan asked you to replace him you've been more nervous than a high schooler for their first dance at the prom!"

"I'm sorry," she said. "But this is a big deal. I don't want to let Dan down."

"You're not going to let him down. Just be yourself out there, and everything will be fine."

"You think?"

"Sure. Hey, movie stars are regular people, too, and they're going to be very much themselves this weekend, just a little get-together of friends."

"Yeah—yeah, I guess you're right," she said, even though she had the distinct impression he was wrong. Stars like Emerald Rhone or Alina Isman were never truly themselves when out in public, and that's what this shindig was, after all: a public affair. Otherwise why was she invited? If this was friends and family only, would Emerald have invited Dan?

No, this was a public event, and Odelia was going to be subjected to the same scrutiny as the rest of them, which meant she needed to look her absolute and stunning best.

"Besides," Chase went on, "it's not as if we're going to be the center of attention. We'll just be flies on the wall—the guests no one pays attention to."

She nodded, and willed herself to relax her death grip on the steering wheel. Usually Dan handled these high-profile get-togethers. They were important networking opportunities. But more and more he was pushing Odelia to take over for him—introducing her into the world of celebrities.

"With so many famous stars there, we're going to blend right in," Chase said. "And isn't that the whole point? For you to have access to these people and still be able to write your articles? You're not the star, babe—you just have to mingle with the stars so you can write about them."

She was nodding in agreement. "And that's my strength as a reporter. Not to stand out too much, while at the same time earning the real stars' trust."

"Hey, those stars don't appreciate it if some reporter steals the limelight. So frankly speaking the plainer and less flashy we both look, the better."

She laughed. He was right. Stars hate to be upstaged. She darted a quick look at him. He was looking his usual handsome self. Dressed in tan slacks, aquamarine button-down and penny loafers, he could have featured in a Ralph Lauren ad for menswear. She'd opted for a simple floral-pattern summer dress and still felt underdressed for the occasion. But he was right. They weren't the stars, and they shouldn't try to look like stars, either.

"So about Max and Dooley," she said. "You know I couldn't take them. Dan was very specific about that. No cats allowed."

"I'm sure Emerald would have made an exception. They're housebroken."

"It's not that. Emerald is allergic to cats."

"And yet she's always photographed lugging that little mutt around."

"That's different. A person can be allergic to cats and not to dogs."

"Hey—your cats, your rules, babe."

"And even if Emerald wasn't allergic, it just wouldn't be practical. If I take Max and Dooley, I'd have to take Brutus and Harriet, too, and their bowls and litter boxes, and it would just turn into a whole production and for what? Just so they can spend the weekend at Emerald's? No, they'll be fine with Mom."

She was feeling a little guilty about leaving her cats behind. They were rarely separated for even one night, and now she was going away for a whole weekend. But it was a little impractical, and she could hardly impose on Emerald, who was one of the world's biggest stars. It was a miracle they'd been invited in the first place, so showing up with four cats, their litter boxes, bowls, bags of cat food, favorite blankets, pillows and toys would be nuts.

They'd be fine at her mother's place, who'd make sure they were fed and taken care of. Besides, she was sure the cast of *Big Little Secrets* would all bring their own pets—all dogs—and create trouble for Max and the others.

She wouldn't want Max and the others facing off with a pack of wild Maltipoos, Yorkshire Terriers, Chihuahuas, Shih Tzus or Brussels Griffons!

Chapter Three

That night, the four of us were lying on the couch Marge reserved for us in the family room, while she and her husband Tex and her mother Vesta were watching a movie. It had been Gran's turn to choose the movie, and she had picked one of her favorite ones: *Pearl Harbor,* now playing on the flatscreen.

"I really can't imagine what you see in that movie, Mom," said Marge.

"Shush," said Gran. The big kissing scene between Ben Affleck and Kate Beckinsale was coming up, and she didn't want to miss a thing, as the song goes.

Marge's brother Uncle Alec, a frequent guest, was already half asleep, and Tex looked about to doze off, too. They weren't too big on kissing scenes.

Marge, who'd wanted to watch *The Bachelorette,* didn't look happy either.

"It's flyboys!" said Gran. "How can you not like flyboys?"

"I like flyboys as much as the next fly girl," said Marge, "but what I don't like is watching the same movie over and over and over and over again."

"It's a classic!" said Gran. "Just like *Titanic*! You never get bored with *Titanic,* do you? So?"

Marge shook her head. This was not an argument she was going to win. "You guys are awfully quiet," she said instead, addressing the four of us.

Reading from left to right there was Dooley, yours truly, Brutus and Harriet. Harriet strictly speaking belongs to Marge, Brutus to Chase, and Dooley to Gran, but basically we consider the entire Poole family our home.

"They're not happy Odelia didn't take them along," said Gran without looking away from her flyboys' exploits. "And quite frankly neither am I."

"Emerald is allergic to cats. Some people are," said Marge.

"You mean to tell me that Emerald Rhone, reigning queen of Tinseltown, is allergic to cats? I don't believe it."

"That's what Odelia told me."

Gran was shaking her head and muttering something under her breath. She wasn't a big fan of people who weren't big fans of cats.

"She can't help it if she's allergic, can she?" said Marge. "It's a medical thing."

"Medical thing my ass. I'll bet she's faking it."

"That's crazy. Why would she fake being allergic to cats?"

"For the attention! These Hollywood types all have imaginary medical conditions. I'll bet she's not allergic to cats at all, just making a big thing out of it. And meanwhile poor Max is deprived the company of his favorite human."

"I like to think we're all Max's favorite humans," said Marge a little huffily.

"Cats like Max attach themselves to one human for life, and in his case that human happens to be Odelia—so tough luck for the rest of us."

"Well," said Marge. "I'm sure you're just imagining it. Max loves all of us exactly the same. Isn't that right, Max?"

To be honest I wasn't in the mood to put Marge's mind at ease that I liked her very much, too, thank you very much. Gran was right. I missed my human. Yeah, I know what you're all thinking: cats don't miss their humans. Cats are independent creatures and they don't care if their human lives or dies and yadda yadda yadda. Well, let me tell you that's all fake news, people. Cats get attached to their humans just as much as the next canine, or at least this particular feline does. And I was just wondering what Odelia was doing at that moment when Marge's phone sang out the theme song from the reboot of *Beverly Hills, 90210.*

"Hey, honey, have you settled in all right?" she asked.

"Ask her about the sheets," said Gran, nudging her daughter. "And ask her about the food. Oh, and ask her if it's true that Emerald's skin looks like a drumhead from all those facelifts and those gallons and gallons of Botox."

"Have you met Emerald yet?" asked Marge, ignoring her mother. "You have? Ooh, how exciting! So what is she like? Is she nice?"

And while the adults in the room prattled on, and Ben Affleck was fighting the good fight over in Europe while his best friend was hitting on his girl, I noticed for the first time that my compadres were all very quiet indeed.

"Is everything all right?" I asked, giving Brutus a slight nudge.

"Oh, Max," was his response. It didn't sound like he was all right at all.

I cut a glance to Harriet, who merely rolled her expressive eyes at me.

"What's going on with him?" I mouthed.

"Don't ask!" she mouthed back.

"What's going on with Brutus, Max?" asked Dooley now.

"I don't know. I asked him and he wouldn't say."

"Ask him if it's menopause," said Dooley.

"Menopause is a human thing, Dooley."

"Oh?"

"It's not menopause," said Harriet. "It's worse—much worse."

"Worse?" asked Dooley. "What could be worse than menopause?"

"Like I said, menopause is a human thing and doesn't—"

"Cancer!" said Dooley suddenly. "Do you have cancer, Brutus?"

Dooley has a tendency to think that whenever someone doesn't feel A-Okay, it's because they are suffering from cancer. Or, apparently, menopause.

"No, it's not cancer," said Brutus gruffly. "Though sometimes I wish it was."

That sounded ominous. And now, of course, I was more curious than ever.

"He misses Odelia," said Dooley knowingly. He patted Brutus on the paw. "Don't worry, buddy," he said loudly. "She'll be back before you know it!"

Brutus merely grumbled something. It didn't sound overly friendly.

So it wasn't Odelia either. So what could it be?

"I know!" said Dooley. "Of course! How silly of me. You miss Chase, don't you?" He patted the butch black cat on the paw again. "Don't worry, buddy. Chase will be back before you know it. And I'm sure he misses you too."

"I don't miss Chase, and will you stop touching me!"

"Touchy," Dooley muttered.

"If you have to know..." Harriet began.

"Don't you dare," growled Brutus.

"They're your friends, Brutus. They have a right to know."

"No, they don't!"

"Brutus is having trouble with—"

"Stop talking now!"

"His inner male," Harriet finally finished.

Dooley and I stared at the big cat. Whatever I'd expected, it wasn't this.

"I'm sorry, what did you say?" I asked.

"Brutus feels that maybe he's a female trapped in a male's body, and now he's thinking about talking to someone."

I stared from Brutus to Harriet and back. "I don't get it," I said.

"Me neither," said Dooley. "Who's inside Brutus's body talking to him?"

"Nobody!" Brutus exploded. "It's just that... have you never wondered if you were who you thought you were or maybe you were really someone else?"

I blinked. "Um, you lost me there," I said.

"Me, too," said Dooley.

"I mean, society has all these expectations of a male cat.

Just look at me. I'm butch, I'm handsome, I'm strong—your stereotypical hard-nosed male, right?"

"Uh-huh," I said. "Go on."

"Well, what if deep down I'm a tender-hearted, sweet-natured... female?!"

Dooley and I shared a look, then burst into a hearty bout of laughter.

"I knew it!" cried Brutus, and jumped down from the couch. "I knew you two wouldn't understand!" And off he went, slinking away with a panther-like grace—or was it a pantheress?

"Wait, he's not kidding?" I said.

"Nuh-uh," said Harriet. "And the worst part is, now he's trying to convince me that maybe deep down I'm a male, and not a female as I always thought."

"But you *are* a female," I said.

"Duh," she said.

"You're probably the most female feline of all the female felines around," said Dooley deferentially.

She permitted herself a slight smile. "Thanks, Dooley. That's very sweet of you to say."

I was still reeling. "So when did Brutus..."

"Figure he might be a female trapped in a male body? After he saw a documentary on the subject," said Harriet. "It's gotten him all confused. And the worst part? He's lost all interest in me!"

"That *is* bad," Dooley agreed, though he didn't sound sorry. Dooley has always had a crush on Harriet, and I had the distinct impression he wouldn't mind Brutus turning into a female so he could take his place by Harriet's side.

And we would probably have explored the topic a lot further, if not suddenly Marge thrust her phone to my ear and I heard the most beautiful sound in the world: the voice of my human asking me how I was holding up.

EPILOGUE

Odelia was seated in her usual chair, only her right leg had been propped up on a second chair. She'd twisted her ankle, but she'd assured us she was going to be just fine.

"I don't like how Odelia keeps getting hurt by these murderous people," said Dooley, who was lying next to me on Marge and Tex's porch swing.

"I don't like it either," I said. "But I guess that's the nature of the job."

"What, reporter?"

"No, sleuth."

"I think she's a great sleuth," said Brutus. "In fact she's probably the greatest sleuth ever since they invented sleuths."

"Nobody invented sleuths, Brutus," said Harriet.

"Of course they did. Or do you think there have always been sleuths? Someone must have been the first sleuth, and that person invented sleuthing."

"Well, I don't care who was the first one, I just wish Odelia would be more careful and not fall down stairs or almost get shot or stabbed or whatever."

"She's promised to be more careful," I said. "And I'm sure Chase will make sure she keeps her promise."

Chase had been at Odelia's every beck and call, catering to her every need, and fussing over her at every turn. It had ingratiated him to us even more, if that was possible.

"I still can't believe that Jeb's daughter was behind this whole thing," said Harriet. "She seemed like such a nice little poppet."

"A nice little murderous poppet," Brutus growled.

Fae had made a full confession and would soon appear in court. It was hard to believe that someone so young could commit an act so atrocious, but there it was.

"I heard that she used to hurt cats," said Harriet.

"Where did you hear that?" asked Brutus.

"Hurt cats?" said Dooley, stunned. "But that's terrible!"

"Tigger told me, and he heard it from Buster, the hairdresser's cat, who heard it from one of the customers. Yes, she hurt little kittens when she was only a little girl herself. She was in therapy for a while, after her parents found out."

"Obviously it didn't stick," said Brutus.

"But that's awful!" Dooley cried.

"Yeah, that wasn't very nice," Harriet admitted.

"Not nice! How can anyone hurt a little kitten!" Dooley wailed.

Harriet had finally broken down and had accepted the kittens into her heart. A little late, though, for they'd gone home with Elsie.

"I need that video, Alec," Gran was saying.

"You can't have it! That video is police property now, not to mention evidence. You can't just post police evidence on your blog."

"Flog, not blog."

"Vlog, Gran," said Odelia. "Not flog."

"Vlog, flog, who cares! I need that video. I'll get millions of followers if I can just post that video, and—"

"And finally trump Scarlett? You should be ashamed of yourself, Mom," said Marge. "Showing such a horrible video just to get more likes and followers. That's just wrong."

Gran seemed taken aback by this, then she nodded. "You know what, Marge, I think you may have a point."

"Of course I have a point! If you post that video you're no better than Scarlett who posts videos of her cleavage just to attract more views, or those women shaking their butts."

"Murder isn't the same as cleavage or butts," said Tex, muttering his two cents. "Just saying."

He was flipping burgers on the grill, and was actually getting pretty good at it, too.

"I still think it's amazing how Odelia caught that girl," said Chase, who still hadn't gotten over the fact that his first hunch had been wrong and that Odelia was right.

"Intuition, honey," said Marge, giving the burly cop's shoulder a squeeze. "More potato salad?"

"Yes, ma'am," said Chase, as Marge ladled a big helping onto his plate.

"And there's chocolate cake for dessert, so leave some space in that stomach of yours."

"Oh, the kid's got a big stomach," said Uncle Alec, slapping his own voluminous belly.

"You know?" said Gran. "Maybe I should give this whole flogging thing a rest. You're right, Marge. Posting all that horrible stuff online just to get a couple more views is just not right. Maybe from now on I'll post videos of cute kittens instead. How about that?"

"That's the spirit," said Uncle Alec, raising his glass in a toast.

"So what's going to happen to Jeb now?" asked Marge.

"Looks like he's cleaning up his act," said Odelia. "There

may even be a reconciliation in the works between him and Helena, who's pretty devastated after what their daughter did."

"She knew, didn't she?"

"Fae told her just before we arrived for that second interview. That's why she was crying so hard. She knew but didn't know what to do. If she told the police, her daughter was going to jail. And if she didn't, her ex-husband was. Either way, she was in hell."

"I can only imagine what that must be like," said Marge. "For your own daughter to do something so horrific, so evil." She shivered.

"Let's not talk about terrible stuff like that anymore," said Gran. "Let's focus on the good stuff and forget about murder and mayhem for a moment." She raised her own glass. "To Odelia. The finest sleuth in Hampton Cove, maybe even the entire county."

"Odelia," said the others, and all drank to my human's health.

"Pity we can't toast her," said Dooley.

"We can take good care of her," I said. "That's all she needs."

"You know," said Harriet. "I have an idea."

Uh-oh. "Yes?" I said tentatively.

"Why don't we suggest to Odelia that she adopt three new kittens. We can name them Bim 2, Bam 2 and Bom 2, and we'll all take care of them together."

Dooley and Brutus and I shared a look, then we all shook our heads.

"As much as I love Bim, Bam and Bom," said Dooley, "I think four cats is enough."

"Agreed," Brutus grunted.

"Agreed," I said.

Harriet rolled her eyes. "You guys! First you tell me to

love kittens, and now that I finally do, you tell me not to! You're more fickle than me! And that's saying something."

We all laughed at this, even Harriet.

And then Chase came walking over, and handed us all pieces of fresh burger, and for a few moments the only sound that could be heard was four cats munching on patties, and six humans munching on burgers, while more meat was gently sizzling on the grill.

Suddenly a black cloud rose up from the grill, and Tex shouted, "Darn it! Not again!"

ABOUT NIC

Nic Saint is the pen name for writing couple Nick and Nicole Saint. They've penned novels in the romance, cat sleuth, middle grade, suspense, comedy and cozy mystery genres. Nicole has a background in accounting and Nick in political science and before being struck by the writing bug the Saints worked odd jobs around the world (including massage therapist in Mexico, gardener in Italy, restaurant manager in India, and Berlitz teacher in Belgium).

When they're not writing they enjoy Christmas-themed Hallmark movies (whether it's Christmas or not), all manner of pastry, comic books, a daily dose of yoga (to limber up those limbs), and spoiling their big red tomcat Tommy.

www.nicsaint.com

ALSO BY NIC SAINT

The Mysteries of Max

Purrfect Murder

Purrfectly Deadly

Purrfect Revenge

Box Set 1 (Books 1-3)

Purrfect Heat

Purrfect Crime

Purrfect Rivalry

Box Set 2 (Books 4-6)

Purrfect Peril

Purrfect Secret

Purrfect Alibi

Box Set 3 (Books 7-9)

Purrfect Obsession

Purrfect Betrayal

Purrfectly Clueless

Box Set 4 (Books 10-12)

Purrfectly Royal

Purrfect Cut

Purrfect Trap

Purrfectly Hidden

Purrfect Kill

Purrfect Santa

Purrfectly Flealess

Nora Steel

Murder Retreat

The Kellys

Murder Motel

Death in Suburbia

Emily Stone

Murder at the Art Class

Washington & Jefferson

First Shot

Alice Whitehouse

Spooky Times

Spooky Trills

Spooky End

Spooky Spells

Ghosts of London

Between a Ghost and a Spooky Place

Public Ghost Number One

Ghost Save the Queen

Box Set 1 (Books 1-3)

A Tale of Two Harrys

Ghost of Girlband Past

Ghostlier Things

Charleneland

Deadly Ride

Final Ride

Neighborhood Witch Committee

Witchy Start

Witchy Worries

Witchy Wishes

Saffron Diffley

Crime and Retribution

Vice and Verdict

Felonies and Penalties (Saffron Diffley Short 1)

The B-Team

Once Upon a Spy

Tate-à-Tate

Enemy of the Tates

Ghosts vs. Spies

The Ghost Who Came in from the Cold

Witchy Fingers

Witchy Trouble

Witchy Hexations

Witchy Possessions

Witchy Riches

Box Set 1 (Books 1-4)

The Mysteries of Bell & Whitehouse

One Spoonful of Trouble

Two Scoops of Murder

Three Shots of Disaster

Box Set 1 (Books 1-3)

A Twist of Wraith

A Touch of Ghost

A Clash of Spooks

Box Set 2 (Books 4-6)

The Stuffing of Nightmares

A Breath of Dead Air

An Act of Hodd

Box Set 3 (Books 7-9)

A Game of Dons

Standalone Novels

When in Bruges

The Whiskered Spy

ThrillFix

Homejacking

The Eighth Billionaire

The Wrong Woman

Made in the USA
Monee, IL
11 August 2020

38018692R00132